I0684894

A PRESUMPTION
OF GUILT

A Brett Gatlin Mystery/Romance/Thriller

Vincent J. Sachar

Copyright © 2019 by Vincent J. Sachar
All Rights Reserved
Divont Publishers
ISBN:978-0-9898133-9-6
Vincent J. Sachar, Milton, FL

DEDICATED

To those who strive to uphold one of the most sacred principles in the American criminal justice system that a defendant is innocent until proven guilty.

SPECIAL THANKS

To Gwen, my partner in the work I do as an author and my partner in life

SPOILER ALERT

"A Presumption of Guilt" *is the SECOND Brett Gatlin book I have written. Although it definitely stands alone in its storyline, this book references some things that occurred in the first Gatlin book,* "A Life Unappreciated."

TABLE OF CONTENTS

CHAPTER ONE

Innocence Lost

*S*tupid! *She never should have walked alone on these dark city streets. She knew better. And talk about a terrible time to have forgotten her cell phone. Or did she forget it? She thought for sure she had placed it in her backpack. But, after basketball practice, she searched for it. The phone was not there.*

Mom dropped Kelly Ann off before heading straight to her job to work the night shift. Kelly Ann told her mother that, as usual, she'd be getting a ride home from Jeannette's dad.

"Listen," Jeannette once told her, "my dad picks me up after every practice. I talked with him and he's cool with driving you home every time."

But Jeannette was sick on this night and didn't make it. Kelly Ann reminded herself that it was only about a twelve-block walk to the apartment that she and her mom lived in. But, tonight twelve blocks seemed like twelve miles when there's not one single street lamp, nor one other person in sight. Kelly Ann felt like she was in one of those old western ghost towns—no signs of life anywhere.

But… there was someone else. She could feel it. Someone was lurking nearby. Someone was stalking her. She neither saw nor heard anything to support this, but something inside of her was sending out warnings that someone else was near, watching her, wanting her.

Kelly Ann shivered as she felt the coolness of the wind against her face and body. She started walking faster but chose not to run. She didn't want the hidden stranger to know that she was aware of his presence. It might cause him to attack.

She wanted her Mom so badly right now. Rasping breaths, a rapid pulse, the sounds of her heartbeats pounding in her ears, she fought to maintain control of her emotions. Even as tears fell from her eyes, she encouraged herself that each step she took brought her closer to home, closer to that place of refuge.

With two blocks to go, her confidence soared that she was going to make it. Hah, guess this had been nothing more than an overactive imagination gone south. Soon, very soon, she'd be kicking her shoes off, phoning her Mom to let her know that she was home, and preparing to settle in for the night.

But that was not to be the case at all. He appeared out of nowhere. He moved so swiftly, so powerfully, that she never even had an opportunity to scream. A curtain of blackness draped over her consciousness. She was unaware, when he placed her in the back seat of a car, that he was taking her to a place from which there was no return.

❧

The morning sun winked as it began its slow ascension in the eastern sky. An orange glow radiated over the surface of the Blackwater River as it flowed through downtown Milton. Brett Gatlin had not been in the Florida Panhandle all that long and already the river ushered in a sense of peace every time he gazed at it.

The aroma of his steaming cup of black coffee beckoned him to take another sip. Brett turned his head, stared out the second-story office window, and sighed. Could it be that his life was beginning to take on a pattern of normalcy? Even now, he sometimes found it difficult to believe that he was no longer the target of a nationwide search by law enforcement officials—all operating under an edict to capture him dead or alive.

Milton, nestled within the Florida Panhandle, some twenty-three miles northeast of Pensacola, was incorporated in 1844, making it one of the oldest cities in Florida. The county seat of Santa Rosa County, Milton is also home to Naval Air Station Whiting Field, one of the Navy's two primary bases that provide training for U.S Navy, U.S. Marine Corps, Coast Guard, and Air Force student pilots, along with those of several allied nations. With its downtown situated along the banks of the Blackwater River and listed on the National Register of historic places, the city is rich in history and culture.

Brett first visited the area with Roger Clark, his closest friend, and a former Air Force pilot who flew the F-22 Raptor.

"I did my initial pilot training here at Whiting," Roger said. "I also did a lot of canoeing in my free time. Milton's known as the Canoe Capital of Florida. It has waterways with names like *Coldwater, Blackwater,* and *Sweetwater* that flow through the town. You're talking about a laid-back lifestyle, opportunities for fishing and boating, and a country atmosphere."

Brett Gatlin had been an outstanding student and athlete throughout high school in Antioch, Tennessee. At six feet two inches with sandy brown hair, brown eyes, and a well-defined handsome face, Gatlin was one of those guys who had it all. He played football, basketball, and baseball and graduated with academic honors. Afterwards, he graduated *summa cum laude* from Vanderbilt Law School. He was entertaining lucrative offers from top national law firms and Fortune 500 corporations when his younger brother Derek's heroin addiction and gang-related murder caused Brett to alter his life plans and become a DEA Federal Agent. After undergoing the rigorous training to become a special agent, Gatlin added to his stature by becoming one of the less than half successful candidates for the DEA's Rapid Response Team, now replaced by Special Response Teams. Brett Gatlin went one step further when he agreed to be one of six special agents to comprise the most elite DEA special ops team in history. The undercover team, named *Subterraneo,* had additional training provided by the FBI, CIA, and Navy SEALs.

At thirty-three years old, Gatlin was still the handsome, fit man who appeared to have so much going in his favor. But there was a portion of his persona shrouded in mystery, tucked away from the eyes of others. Four years of undercover work as a federal agent where one slipup could be fatal, combined with months as a fugitive eluding law enforcement officers nationwide, helped construct these hidden walls. Deep inner wounds and scars from the betrayals he suffered festered within him. The man left behind in their wake was still in need of healing and repair.

Yet, Brett had moved on. He was now a member of the Florida Bar. His law office was located on the banks of the Blackwater River.

Brett's office door was open, but Betty Jo Felton tapped lightly on it before entering. Betty Jo was one of Brett's two full-time employees. A thirty-four-year-old single-mother divorcee with a twelve-year-old daughter, Betty Jo wore several hats. She sat at the reception desk, coordinated appointments, handled the office administrative tasks, and filed legal documents with the courts. She worked hard to keep the office running smoothly.

"Good morning, Boss," she said with a smile. "Got the morning mail here. Nothing much. You got another communication from that reporter wanting to do an interview. Guess since you don't take her calls or respond to her emails, she resorted to snail mail in trying to reach you."

Brett did not respond, and Betty Jo did not press things. She knew that Brett was not interested in communicating any further with the press.

~

Gatlin's other full-time employee was his best friend, Roger Clark. While Brett was studying and sitting for the Florida Bar, Clark underwent training as a private investigator, leading to his current role in working with Gatlin.

Clark first met Gatlin when Brett was battling through the most distressful time of his life. For months, Gatlin was front-page news, falsely accused of betraying his oath as a DEA Federal Agent. Law enforcement agencies and the nationwide media claimed that Brett was responsible for the deaths of some twenty-nine American federal agents and Mexican national police officers. Clark teamed up with Brett in an effort to prove Gatlin's innocence. The two had become inseparable ever since. After he was proven innocent, Brett resigned from the DEA.

At forty-two years old, Roger's body, standing at five feet eleven, was lean and tight. His brown wavy hair extended past his ears and added to the relaxed, youthful look the man bore. His facial hair sported some light silvery patches. His green eyes conveyed a message of warmth and intelligence. After serving his country as a pilot of what is considered to be an aircraft unprecedented in its air combat capabilities and unmatched by any known or projected fighter, Roger figured he'd already faced life's greatest challenges.

Roger was currently dating Adriana Dominguez, a native Brazilian, who was employed as an international flight attendant on flights primarily from Orlando to a major Brazilian city. Addie was born in Porto Alegre, the capital city of the Brazilian state of Rio Grande do Sul.

"Porto Alegre," Adriana told Roger, "has the highest life quality in the country, is located in a rich metropolis, and has a literacy rate of ninety-seven percent."

"Sounds awesome," Roger said.

"You know, Porto Alegre was founded in 1772," Adriana continued.

"That is even before America declared its independence from the British," Roger said.

Adriana smiled and hugged Roger.

"I should like to take you there to visit one day," she said.

Addie chose to live in Pensacola and travel to Orlando when on-duty because her ailing mother and an aunt both lived in Pensacola.

Rog arrived for the day wearing a New Orleans Saints cap and holding a Styrofoam cup of coffee. In a dissimilar way and for differing reasons, Roger found his new career and move to the Florida Panhandle to be rejuvenating. He moved to the area when Gatlin did.

"When I was flying the Raptor," Roger once told Brett, "I felt an adrenaline rush and excitement every time I got in the cockpit. It gave my life purpose and meaning. By the time you and I met, I was struggling to redefine my life. You can drink just so much beer, play just so much poker, and wager on just so many sporting events," Roger said with a chuckle.

"Coming back to this area is like traveling full circle with my life. I loved it in Milton and Santa Rosa County when I was training at Whiting and always hoped I'd end up here again."

Roger purchased a condo in Pensacola. Brett had a home in Milton. Both men felt as if they were starting life all over again.

Both men were.

⌒

The shadowy figure passed by his bedroom window in the blackness of the night. Tonight, the stalker would not take the next steps to fulfill his commitment. He was a careful man who studied and planned, even to a state of perfection, before he made his move. Taking another's person's life was not a flippant thing to him, despite the fact that he did it for a living. He regarded the term "hit man" as a cheap title used by those who did not understand the art or profession in which he was engaged.

Besides, the folks that hired him did not merely want the man dead. Before that final act, they wanted Brett Gatlin to suffer, to spend his every hour looking over his shoulder. They wanted him to experience depths of fear he had never before known.

The man continued to study and calculate all he needed to know about Gatlin's residence. He would do the same with Gatlin's law office. He'd follow the man for a while. This assignment had all the makings of a most enjoyable time. He intended to savor every moment before he completed his mission and ended Brett Gatlin's life.

CHAPTER TWO

Innocent or Guilty

Roger and Brett began each day by reviewing the cases that Brett was handling, the progress they had made, and a checklist of things to be done. Roger called it their cockpit checklist. To Brett, it was their covert mission strategy update. In their own way, each of these men were free spirits who were not afraid to improvise or take on something new. Yet, Brett and Roger also possessed a discipline and deep sense of organization.

Roger sat down, placed his cup on Brett's desk, and fist-bumped his friend.

"Hey, man," Roger said, "Betty Jo tells me you got the charges against old Lester Washington dropped."

"Yeah, it's a done deal. I was about ready to leave the office yesterday when I got a call from Judge Maulten. I ended up with an end-of-the day conference with Maulten and Assistant DA Purdy. And, thanks to you, Rog, we were able to punch enough holes in the DA's case to get all the charges against Lester dropped. They were railroading the old man. The DA's office thought they had some easy pickings pinning those burglaries on an old African-American homeless guy."

Roger laughed.

"Man, ain't that the truth. Those charges were bogus from the get-go. And the police and DA either knew it or flat out didn't care all that much about it. Let me tell you, Brett, if you hadn't agreed to represent Washington *pro bono,* I'm convinced the old dude would be spending some serious undeserved time behind bars even now."

Brett took another sip of his coffee. Its pungent aroma filled his nostrils.

"Lester Washington is the kind of person we had in mind when we opened this practice. I believe Kerry is smiling down at us even now."

The mention of Kerry Anderson generated both a warmth and sadness within the two men. Kerry was a Washington Post reporter who was the first and only major journalist to question the accusations that had an entire nation believing in Gatlin's guilt.

"Kerry helped save my life," Brett said on more than one occasion. "She used her position as a reporter to stand up publicly when no one else in the media would. Kerry had the courage to risk her job, her reputation, her safety, if necessary, in order to pursue the truth. I'm telling you, if she believed that someone was being falsely charged with a crime, Kerry would do anything and everything to assist that person."

Gatlin paused, lifted his coffee mug, and took another sip. He peered over the mug and made eye contact with Roger.

"Of course, I could say much the same about you, Rog. I don't know where I'd be if it hadn't been for you."

Roger blushed a bit, lifted a pen from Brett's desk, and twirled it in his hands.

"Aw, I just needed someone to drink a few beers with from time-to-time."

The two men laughed.

Brett and Roger met completely by chance when Brett stepped into a downtown Norfolk, Virginia bar. Roger recognized Brett as the fugitive from the law. Roger had been following the news stories about Gatlin and found himself more aligned with Kerry Anderson's articles. He helped Brett evade the police that night and assisted in proving Gatlin's innocence.

When Brett decided to practice law, he promised to watch out for anyone whom he believed to be innocent but were being rushed to judgment. Roger Clark was totally onboard with that perspective.

"I know what it's like to have your life, your personal integrity, all ripped away while you're defenseless to fight against those who've put you in that position," Brett told a Washington Post reporter. It was the only interview he gave after what he had gone through. That was when he revealed that he was dedicating his new law practice to the memory of Kerry Anderson. The national media picked up his interview.

"Kerry's newspaper, *The Washington Post,* was the only segment of the media willing to take a closer look at me and the charges levied against me. And, even after Kerry started posting her articles, no one else jumped on board. Way I see it, I owe no one else anything," Brett said.

"You won't get an argument from me on that," Roger said. Roger Clark reached over for another fist-bump with Brett. "People with the courage to make their own judgments and take a stand are few and hard to find," Roger said.

Clark picked up his cup and took another sip of coffee before speaking again.

"Hey, changing the subject here, I guess you heard a young girl was abducted yesterday evening over in Tallahassee."

"Yeah," Gatlin said. "It's the kind of thing that makes you sick."

"From what they're saying," Roger said, "the girl, Kelly Ann Lauren, age sixteen, was apparently walking home from a high school basketball practice at Milford Fulbright High School. Horrible. And from what I could gather, Tallahassee PD doesn't seem to know much more right now."

Betty Jo Felton knocked twice on the office door before entering. She was shaking her head and rubbing her hands together.

"They just found the body of that young girl in Tallahassee. I can't imagine what I'd do if anything ever happened to Janie," Betty Jo said, referring to her daughter.

Betty Jo paused and took in a deep breath before speaking again. She fought hard to maintain her composure.

"Hey, Brett, we've got a lady here. She's like super-distraught. Says she just drove in from Tallahassee. Didn't even call ahead. Just jumped in her car and drove straight here. She says she needs to see you right away."

Brett and Roger looked at each other, then turned towards Betty to hear what else she had to say.

"She says the police came and questioned her brother. Says he's a person of interest in last night's abduction of that young girl."

CHAPTER THREE

Borderline

Gatlin guesstimated the woman's age to be somewhere in her late-forties to early-fifties. She was a short woman standing at five feet two inches and carried a few extra pounds generated by childbirth and the passage of time. She had a pretty face with prominent dimples and blue eyes. Her red lipstick was thick and alluring. A hint of perfume entered the room with her. Her blonde hair was short and well-styled. Her clothes, the jewelry she wore, and her general demeanor all sent a message that Jocelyn McCallister was a woman of considerable wealth.

As she sat in one of the office chairs, Jocelyn continued to twist the rings on her fingers, none of which was a wedding ring. She shifted in her seat in a futile effort to get comfortable. Everything changed as the woman prepared to speak. She took a deep breath, made strong eye contact with Brett, and gave a curt nod. Jocelyn McCallister had come with a set goal in mind and she was determined to give it her best shot.

"Mister Gatlin, I read the Washington Post interview article about you and your law practice. You say you've dedicated your legal practice to people unjustly charged with a crime or otherwise unfairly oppressed. The moment that the police came and questioned Chuck, I knew that you were the lawyer we need."

The "Chuck" that Jocelyn referred to was her brother, Charles Richardson. The Tallahassee Police questioned Chuck in connection with the abduction of Kelly Ann Lauren. Since then, the police discovered Kelly Ann's body in a wooded area just outside the city limits of Tallahassee.

Roger was in the room with Brett and Jocelyn McCallister as this was merely a preliminary discussion with someone other than the potential client and did not generate issues of attorney/client privilege. He was listening closely as the woman spoke.

"My brother is innocent," McCallister said. "I tell you, he didn't have anything to do with that girl. He would never do that. He's done nothing wrong."

Jocelyn turned towards Roger, then back towards Brett. Her tone was softer now and her lips quivered. She glanced up at the ceiling, then squeezed her eyes shut. She shrugged and nodded her head.

"Look, I'm not saying that he's some kind of angel. Chuck's had a few incidents in the past. We're talking about things like indecent exposure and some girl with a ridiculous claim that Chuck tried to rape her. But that was years ago when he was much younger and was drinking heavily. Since then, Chuck has changed. He got himself a job as a janitor at the high school where that girl attended. He quit drinking, cut down on his smoking, even goes to church with me and my daughter when she's home from college.

I'm telling you, Mister Gatlin, Chuck would never do something like this."

Tears began to drip from Jocelyn's eyes and slide down her cheeks. She opened her purse and began rummaging through it, but Roger reached for a box of tissues nearby and handed them to her. She gently dabbed her eyes.

Brett was frowning. A slight chill passed through his body. Chuck's past improprieties were certain to generate a negative impact should the police heighten their focus upon this man.

Nevertheless, Brett leaned forward. He spoke softly while keeping his gaze on the distraught woman.

"Miss McCallister, based upon what you're saying, your brother has not been formally charged with anything. Questioning your brother in no way indicates that he's a prime suspect.

The police will question everyone who works at the school or may have had any contact with the girl or her family. They're going to need solid evidence before they charge your brother or anyone else with murder."

Brett smiled and tapped his fingers on his desk.

"I'm sure you have a great deal of love for your brother," Brett continued, "and that you believe that he has not committed this horrendous crime. And, believe me, he will need that kind of support from someone like you. But, let me remind you, the fact that your brother works at that school and may have some check marks against him in the past is not enough to... "

Jocelyn interrupted.

"Mr. Gatlin, I have every reason to believe that once the word spreads that Chuck is a suspect his past will make it easy for the media and the public to assume that he's guilty."

"Miss McCallister," Roger said, "what your saying is true, but on its own it is not enough for an arrest to be made. There's going to have to be compelling evidence linking your brother to the abduction and murder of Kelly Ann Lauren."

"I do understand that, gentlemen," Jocelyn said as she switched her gaze between Brett and Roger, "but that won't stop them from putting some real pressure on Chuck that he will not be able to handle. Chuck is functional, but he is somewhat mentally challenged."

Jocelyn turned back towards Brett Gatlin.

"You men talk about solid evidence, but, tell me Mister Gatlin, was there solid evidence when you were accused of crimes? Was it an open-and-shut case when just about everyone was convinced that you were guilty? To be perfectly honest with you, I'm thinking about my initial impression back when I first heard about you on the news. I figured that you had aided and abetted in the murders of nearly thirty people—government agents, in fact. Yes, I believed that. The media, law enforcement, the public—they all made it sound as if there was no question that you were guilty. So, I just went along with it and assumed you were. And, even though you were proven innocent, did you not pay a heavy price for that? Does it not hang over your head today?"

Gatlin's mouth dropped open. His body was rigid and taut. Yes, he had paid a heavy price, heavier than most people might ever realize. And, yes, the lies spread about him would follow him for the remainder of his life. Jocelyn McCallister was right.

When a person is charged with a major crime that becomes a national sensation, it doesn't matter if he or she is ultimately proven innocent. Some people will believe that the person must have done something wrong to even be charged or were guilty and got away with their crime. The name Brett Gatlin would be associated with betraying his country and responsibility for the deaths of so many innocent government agents. Would there not always be some who questioned why, of all the federal agents and Mexican national police, Gatlin, alone, escaped death that day in the Sonoran Desert?

Brett sat frozen in place as he considered Jocelyn's words. Roger remained silent. He knew that this was Brett's battle. He also knew that it was connected to something that was not totally healed within Brett.

Gatlin reached down, lifted his coffee cup, then placed it back down on his desk. He spoke slowly at first, being careful and precise with his words.

"Miss McCallister," Brett said, "let's regroup here. Your brother is not under arrest. And, I need to be frank with you. If he is arrested... I am not the best person to represent him. There are criminal attorneys with a great deal more experience than me. And, I'm sure that I don't need to tell you, that the murder case of a young local high school student will generate sensationalism greater than you likely can imagine."

Jocelyn McCallister paused. Her pursed her lips, furrowed brow, and the action she took in lifting her purse from the floor all sent a message that she was about to respond to Brett's statement. The sound of her purse zipper being pulled open was followed by a momentary stare back-and-forth at Gatlin and Roger Clark. Then, Jocelyn reached into her purse. Still, without saying a word, she opened her wallet, and withdrew a stack of one-hundred-dollar bills. She laid twenty of them down on the desk. Then, she nodded her head.

"I beg to differ," she said to Gatlin. "I believe you are the perfect person to represent Chuck. I assure you, sir, the more you learn about my brother, the more you will realize that he is one of those people for whom you have dedicated your practice of law."

Brett did not respond nor reach for the money sitting on his desk. Roger, again realizing it was Brett's move, remained silent.

Jocelyn McCallister broke the silence.

"All I'm asking is that you remain available to us should the police do anything to follow up with my brother. I don't want us to ever be caught unprepared. Will you do that? If you come to Tallahassee, I'd want you to speak with Chuck. You can then make a judgment as to whether you're willing to represent him. If you decide not to, you can keep the money as payment for your troubles. Should you decide to represent Chuck, that can serve as an initial retainer. I expect your fees will be quite elaborate should you take this case. I assure you that I am fully capable of payment."

Brett looked over towards Roger, who shrugged, placed his hands palms-up, and nodded.

"Okay, Miss McCallister," Brett said. "If you hear from the police again, contact me right away and I'll come and speak with your brother with the understanding that I may opt out from representing him and return this money to you."

The woman sighed. A slight smile appeared momentarily on her face. She sighed deeply.

"Thank you. I appreciate this. Thank you. And, please, gentlemen, call me Jocelyn."

As Brett stared at Jocelyn McCallister, he acknowledged that the woman was not the least bit objective when it came to her brother. Her opinion that he was innocent would never be something Gatlin could rely on. At this point in time, Brett did not know whether the police questioned Charles Richardson simply because he worked at Fulbright High School or whether they had a more compelling reason to do so?

Roger escorted Jocelyn to Betty Jo who would have Jocelyn fill out some forms and provide all of her contact information.

Brett sat at his desk, turned towards the window, and stared out at the flowing river. He might have just agreed to meet with the man who kidnapped and killed a young girl.

CHAPTER FOUR

Closure Time

"Hah! Let's see you top that one, Gatlin," Roger said as he stepped from the tee following his best drive of the day.

The two men were playing a round of golf at Milton's Tanglewood Golf and Country Club—the course where they say famed pro golfer Bubba Watson first learned to play.

Roger was good, Brett, always an outstanding athlete, was better. But, golf scores and competition between the two was of no significance on this day. The ability to take a day off and relax together was primary.

Brett drove his ball from the tee. It carried straight and true down the fairway at a distance beyond Roger's drive. Roger laughed. On their next shots, each man landed on the green. As the two men approached the eighth green, Roger paused, pulled his putter from his golf bag, and walked up to Brett.

"Okay, Amigo, I've been patient. Tell me what's going on in that brain of yours?"

Brett spun his head towards Roger. He stared at him, was about to deny that anything was on his mind, then paused. He realized that would be nothing more than an exercise in futility.

Roger was more than a trained investigator. He was the person closest to Brett Gatlin.

"You don't miss a trick, do you, Rog?" Brett laughed. Then, everything changed. His facial features bore no expression. When he next spoke, his voice was devoid of emotion. He continually refused to look at Roger.

"I think that I'm ready now, Rog. At least, I hope that I am. I've been doing a great deal of thinking lately, even though I realize this is a decision fraught with emotion that cannot be based entirely in the mind. We both said when the time came, I'd know."

Brett stood silently, staring at the ground. Finally, he lifted his head, looked at Roger, and spoke just above a whisper.

"I-I just can't keep living in my yesterdays, Rog. Those days are history. I can't change a single thing about them. I would give anything if I could, but that's not possible."

Roger needed no explanation, no clarification as to what Brett was talking about. He knew in an instant. Despite the seriousness of the moment, Roger tipped his head back and turned his face to the sky. He thrust a fist upwards.

"I've waited for this moment, Brett. I believe it's part of the full closure you need and deserve. And, beyond that, it will be a genuine tribute to Kerry and her family."

Brett bowed his head.

"I've really struggled, Rog. Kerry and I never had a chance to establish a relationship. Yet, I still feel attached to her, bound to her. When will that ever end?"

Roger paused for a moment and put a hand on Brett's shoulder. He nodded his head and spoke softly.

"It ends when you decide that it's okay to start living again, Brett."

Kerry Anderson's family resided in Elkhart, Indiana. Sometime after the news was released that Brett had been found innocent of all previous charges against him, he received a letter from Kerry's older sister, Tara. In addition to rejoicing in Brett's vindication, Tara mentioned that Kerry had shared her strong feelings for Brett with her older sister. Tara invited Brett to come visit the family and meet everyone. Then, when Brett conducted an interview stating that his new law practice would be dedicated to Kerry and all that she stood for, Tara had a florist deliver an African Violet, Kerry's favorite flower, with a card congratulating Brett on his new endeavor. She thanked him for honoring her sister and reminded him that he was always welcome to visit their family in Elkhart.

Brett's heart was shattered when he lost Kerry before he ever started a romantic relationship with her. Now, he was ready to take another step and meet her family.

"You don't know how happy I am to hear you say what you just did, Brett. It's like music to my ears. Heck, I might just let you win this round of golf as evidence of how happy I am."

Brett and Roger laughed. Brett already had a four-stroke lead after seven holes.

"Rog, there's one additional thing. I-I really want you to come with me to meet Kerry's family. She was your friend, also."

Roger smiled and tapped Brett on his shoulder.

"No, Brett. Maybe... afterwards, someday down the road. But, right now... well, it seems to me this is something you need to do on your own."

Brett nodded his head and smiled. He placed a hand on Roger's shoulder. The two men embraced each other. Tears flooded their eyes. Then, just as quickly, their tears turned to laughter as they high-fived each other. They were glad that it was a slow day at Tanglewood and there were no other golfers close by them. They wouldn't have been able to explain why they were dancing around on the eighth green.

∽

As his plane left Pensacola Airport and headed for Chicago's O'Hare, Brett recalled the phone conversation he had several days earlier with Tara Anderson. He inquired about whether they were open to a visit from him. Tara never hesitated. She quickly welcomed Brett and assured him that her parents would also be elated.

Then, Brett and Tara chatted for nearly two hours. Initially they spoke about Kerry. Then, they chatted about a vast number of subjects. Brett learned that Tara, at thirty-two, was one year younger than him. Like Brett, she was an attorney. She earned her Juris Doctor at Notre Dame Law School. She was employed at the civil practice law firm of Graham and Kittrich.

Brett had been a public person of notoriety when he was a fugitive from the law and the center of Kerry Anderson's Washington Post articles. Tara was well-versed on the general subject of Brett Gatlin.

Neither of them had been previously married, although Tara had once been engaged. Tara had never been to Tennessee. Brett had only passed through Indiana when he was running from the law. Tara had never been in Florida's

Panhandle, though she had been to Disneyworld in Orlando, areas of south Florida, and the Keys.

With a stopover at Chicago's O'Hare Airport, Brett could complete his trip to Elkhart, Indiana by plane, train, bus, or by car. He chose to rent a car and drive two hours to his destination. He savored the idea of being alone in a vehicle to prepare himself for what he knew would be an emotional meeting with Kerry's family.

Kerry Anderson was an unfulfilled love. She came into Brett's life as a Washington Post journalist who believed in his innocence when it seemed as if no one else did. Brett was attracted to her, but he and Kerry were working together to prove Brett's innocence. They both resisted the compelling forces that attracted them to each other. Kerry was the love that Brett never openly expressed. They never kissed and never even confessed to each other how they felt. Brett and Kerry never did or said a single thing that openly admitted that they were more than a journalist and fugitive joined together in a fight for justice. And just that quickly, without any advance warning, any opportunity to express their love for each other was forever gone.

As Brett pulled up to the Anderson home, his body was shaking. He had never met any of them. He was in jail at the time of Kerry's funeral.

Kerry's mom, Julia, and her sister, Tara, were at the house when Brett arrived. Kerry's mom, with her warm engaging smile, was the first to greet and hug Brett. When Brett spotted Tara, his body was flooded with a coldness that reached down into the very marrow of his bones. He fought hard against revealing the weakness in his legs and the difficulty to breathe normally that he was having. His heart was racing. He was lightheaded and a threat of nausea was attempting to rise up. Whatever Brett may have anticipated, he never would have expected this.

Kerry had blonde hair and was five feet eight inches tall. Tara's hair was brunette. She was an inch taller than her younger sister had been. But, other than that, the girls could have passed for twins. As Brett stared at Tara, he felt as if he were in the presence of a ghost. Kerry was alive again—same green eyes, same high cheek bones, same heartwarming smile that highlighted her dimples, same jolting impact upon his heart.

Brett sighed in relief, thankful for the additional time he had to recover, when Kerry's father, Edward, entered the house, walked up to Brett, and extended his hand in greeting.

"Mister Gatlin, please forgive me for not being here upon your arrival. Got caught in traffic on my way home from the office," Edward said. "We're all grateful that you were able to come here and be with us. The manner in which you have honored our Kerry has helped all of us to better handle the incredible grief we've suffered over losing her."

Brett regained a sizable portion of his composure and was better able to disguise all that he had just experienced. He smiled and spoke while taking the time to acknowledge everyone in the room. The Anderson family proved to be warm, friendly, intelligent, and engaging—just as Kerry had been. They all sat together in the living room. Brett accepted a glass of Julia Anderson's homemade iced tea.

"Kerry was a once-in-a-lifetime person," Brett began. "The impact she had on my life and the lives of so many others is…

uh… immeasurable. I knew immediately upon meeting her that she was a uniquely special person."

Brett had dinner with the Anderson family at their home before he left to return to his motel for the night. The conversations they had were warm and friendly. They all spent some time talking about Kerry, but they also touched on a number of other less hurtful subjects. There was no doubt that Kerry's willingness to take a stand against what she perceived as injustices was shaped, at least in part, by the influences of her family.

Before Brett left that night, he and Tara agreed to meet for dinner the next day. Tara gave Brett the address of her apartment where he agreed to pick her up and bring her to a local restaurant.

Brett's stomach was churning, his pulse was rapid, and his throat was dry as he drove to his motel. Had he just agreed to a date with Tara? There was no doubt that he and Tara exchanged glances throughout the evening. As she walked outside with him that evening, they stood together on the front porch of the Anderson home. Their eyes met and Brett had to fight against an incredible impulse to kiss Tara goodnight. He was quite sure that she felt the same thing.

CHAPTER FIVE

The Next Page

Brett reached Tara's apartment earlier than the agreed-time, which was something he actually appreciated. He sat in the car making a concerted effort to poise himself before he notified Tara that he had arrived. His thoughts were rampant and covered a broad spectrum.

What in the world is wrong with me? When I was undercover in Special Ops, I was in precarious situations where a mistake on my part could prove to be fatal. Afterwards, I had the entire country searching for me under an edict to capture me dead or alive for a sizeable reward. And here I am intimidated by the fact that I agreed to have dinner with a female? It's dinner—just dinner. Got to pull myself together.

But as he walked towards her apartment, Brett was well aware that having dinner with Kerry's sister had the potential to lead to a whole lot more. He, as the man Kerry loved, represented something special to Tara. She, as her sister's lookalike, already had a profound effect on Brett. He walked up to the door and knocked.

❧

The previous night, Brett made a late-night call from his motel room to Roger. He was surprised by the fact that his throat was dry and his hands were clammy.

"The Andersons are nice people, Rog, no doubt about that. I'm glad that I came here."

"That's great," Roger said. "I had a strong feeling that you would all like each other."

"Yes," Brett answered. "Kerry's mom is an excellent cook and one of those special homemakers. Her dad is a real nice guy. He's a partner in an accounting firm. And Tara, Kerry's sister, is a practicing attorney. It was great just being with the family."

"And?" Roger responded, followed by an initial period of silence.

"And what, Rog? There is no 'and.' They're nice people—a very respectable and friendly family."

Another period of silence followed.

"The 'and' I'm referring to, Brett, doesn't apply to the family. You and I would have both been surprised if they were anything but friendly and respectable. You know what I'm referring to, Bubba. You met Tara. Kerry's sister. How did that go?"

Brett paused before speaking. He was glad that Roger could not see his flushed face. He squinted his eyes. His shaky voice betrayed him when he next spoke.

"Well... yeah... she's... uh... a very pleasant person. No doubt about that. She's... I guess you could say very much like... "

"Like Kerry?" Roger interjected.

Brett was silent for what seemed to be a much longer time than it actually was. Roger said nothing, providing Brett with the opportunity to regroup and say whatever he desired.

"I-I was totally caught off guard, Rog. Tara... looks like, talks like, so reminds me of Kerry. And... it-it's not just the physical similarities. She-she's kind, sweet, intelligent, poised just like... just like Kerry."

Brett stopped speaking and Roger, once again, let the silence prevail.

"I don't know what to think, Rog. I can't use Tara to replace Kerry. That's not fair to anyone. And if I were to begin to establish a relationship with Tara, if she'd even want that, how would I ever know whether I would have done so had I not first met and fallen in love with her sister? I-I... "

This time Roger interrupted.

"Take it easy, Brett. For all you know, had you met Tara first, you would have been attracted to her as you were with Kerry. Chill, my friend. Keep your eyes wide open and let's see what happens."

Brett was softer now.

"Thanks, Rog. Tara and I... well, we're having dinner together tomorrow evening."

"That's great. That's perfect. It'll provide you with more opportunity to see how you feel and let things follow their own course.," Roger said. "Just know that I'm here if you need a listening ear."

Tara opened the door to her apartment and Brett had that same reaction as the previous day. Seeing her again confirmed that yesterday was neither a fluke nor a one-time response. Tara was beautiful, but beyond her outward beauty she possessed an inner radiance that escaped through her lustrous emerald eyes and captivating smile.

When they were seated at a table in a local restaurant, that Tara admitted was one of her favorites, Brett ordered a glass of wine for each of them. They did not take any time glancing at the menu. They were in no hurry tonight. In fact, Brett had already determined that he would give their server an extra-generous tip, since, if all went as he hoped, he and Tara would be there for quite some time.

When their waitress returned, Brett ordered another two glasses of wine and promised that they would be ready soon to order from the menu.

"Tara, there's something I need to ask you. Did you or anyone in your family ever blame me for what happened to Kerry. I mean... if she hadn't gotten involved in defending me... "

"Brett, stop. No. That's not even close. None of us ever blamed you for Kerry's death. Remember, Kerry didn't know you nor had she even met you when she posted her first news story in your defense. No one, including me or you, would have ever been able to convince Kerry to back off once she began to suspect that you were being wrongfully accused. Her decision to get involved had nothing personal to do with you. It had everything to do with the injustices she saw."

Brett sat silently for a moment. He knew that Tara was right. Any personal interest Kerry may have developed with respect to Brett came afterwards.

The silence that followed was awkward. As Brett stared at Tara, the thought flashed through his mind to ask if she was presently seeing anyone. He was thankful that he did not. Tara wondered if Brett thought she was even half as attractive as she found him to be.

There were many words such as these that they never openly expressed with each other, but their smiles and the glint of an undeniable magnetic attraction—something mystical that had taken residence in each of their eyes—spoke volumes.

Beyond the feelings these two were already developing for each other, being together was easy and fun. Brett was captivated by Tara's laugh and her smile, as well as her keen mind. Tara loved Brett's sense of humor and ability to articulate in a way that drew her into anything he talked about. Neither of them knew where things would lead from here. At the moment, they were each enraptured with the time they were presently sharing.

"So, you fly home in the morning, Brett? Do you have a busy schedule at present?"

"Not too bad," Brett said. "I have a few pending matters of litigation, a few more that may or may not reach that level, and some probate work I agreed to handle."

Brett paused, then reached over and placed a hand atop one of Tara's hands for a moment.

"I know that what I'm about to say is awkward and might generate some real discomfort for you," Brett said, "so, please, know that I would never want to offend you."

Tara stared into Brett's eyes. She was anxious to hear whatever he wanted to say, but fearful that this is where he would tell her why they could never have any kind of future together. Her heart was racing. She kept her hands on the table in the hope that Brett would not see her trembling. She considered how ludicrous it was that she went to bed last night wondering whether there was any possibility of a relationship with Brett.

As Tara stared at her dinner companion, she considered telling Brett that she understood that they could never have a romantic relationship. She was not Kerry. And the fact that Brett had loved her younger sister did not provide Tara with a free pass to Brett's heart. Surely, this was best for both of them. They had to move on from the grief of losing Kerry. A relationship based upon the common bond that they both had loved Kerry Anderson was, at best, destined to be short-lived. A foundation like that was simply not solid enough to uphold anything between them. They would both realize that before long.

Tara dropped her head, winced, and prepared herself for the words that would politely, but firmly, close the door to any possibility that the two of them could have a future together.

Brett began speaking despite the lack of eye contact with Tara. As Tara anticipated, his voice was soft and conciliatory. Tara's thoughts ran wild.

Wow! I must have made it so obvious that I'm attracted to this man. Foolish of me. Now, he's getting ready to let me down gently, pacifying me, doing all he can to not embarrass me.

"Tara," Brett said, "I'm sure you realize how difficult it would be to even consider the possibility of anything deeper between you and me."

There it was—the beginning of the "goodbye-speech."

"The fact that we both loved Kerry," Brett continued, "the fact that something special could have, would have, probably should have progressed between me and your sister has nothing to do with anything between you and me."

Tara lifted her head, fought hard to hold back any tears, and nodded in agreement.

"Tara, neither of us in any way could ever serve as a replacement for Kerry. She's gone—gone forever," Brett said. "We can't change that."

Tara could now see the tears that were formed in Brett's eyes and, in that moment, her battle against weeping ended. Tears began to glide slowly down her face.

"I-I un-understand, Brett. I know what you're saying is true."

Tara's heart shifted towards compassion for a man who had been cheated of an enduring love with her sister. It was clear to her that Brett was a good man. She could readily see why Kerry had fallen in love with him. She would work hard to care for Brett as a friend, should he ever need that. She would always be available should he ever desire to share memories.

Brett then reached across the table, gently placed Tara's chin in the palm of his hand and spoke as tears fell from his own eyes.

"I-I d-don't have all the answers. I probably don't even have most of them," Brett said, "but I lost a love that I never had opportunity to explore. I... I don't want t-to do that again.

Maybe, you already believe or will find that I'm not a man you could love, Tara. But I'm willing to take that chance. If there's any possibility that I might be someone you would consider in your life, I'm asking you for that opportunity. I want to see you again."

Tara went from soft gliding tears to sobbing. Then, she smiled, ignored her own tears, leaned her body over towards Brett, and their lips met in a soft kiss.

"I want that, Brett. I want that very much."

CHAPTER SIX

Not Going Away

Before Gatlin's plane touched the tarmac at the Pensacola Airport, he had already convinced himself that both he and Tara had reacted to each other because of the depth of grief they both harbored over the loss of Kerry.

"It's all wrong," Brett told Roger when they were together again at the office. "I can't use Tara as a replacement or substitute for her sister. I would only end up hurting her. She's gone through enough grief. Besides, Tara will likely reach the same conclusion. I am nothing more than someone who reminds her of the sister she loved."

Roger sat silently at first, letting his friend battle through his own emotions. Brett rose from his chair, turned away, and stared out the window at the river that flowed below.

"Kerry's gone, Rog. You told me that I needed to accept that and move on with my life."

Brett turned, stood near the window, and stared back at Roger.

Roger nodded, smiled, then spoke.

"As I recall, Brett, you mentioned that, even though Kerry is gone, you still find yourself attached to her. You were questioning when that would ever end."

Brett nodded, walked back to his chair, and sat down. His head was down. His eyes were focused away from Roger.

"Yes, and you said it ends when I decide that it's okay to start living again."

Roger waited before interrupting the silence once again.

"So, that leaves us with only one question, Brett. Is Tara a part of your yesterdays or your tomorrows?"

⁓

A week and a half had passed since Jocelyn McAllister's visit with Brett and Roger.

"Chuck received a call from Tallahassee PD," Jocelyn said on a call she made to Gatlin. "A detective there wanted Chuck to come in to the station to talk with them. Chuck didn't remember the detective's name. It all happened so fast. I told Chuck to tell the police that he had an attorney and would not speak unless you were present. I followed up on Chuck's behalf and gave the police your name and phone numbers."

"Okay," Gatlin said. "You did well, Jocelyn. I'll head your way to meet with Chuck."

Brett quickly informed Roger and they agreed that Roger would make the two-and-a-half-hour trek to Tallahassee with Brett, although, in order to protect any potential attorney/client privilege, Brett would meet alone with Charles "Chuck" Richardson. Before they even headed towards Tallahassee, Brett approached Roger.

"I've been thinking, Rog. How about you give Wireless a call and have him run some background checks on Richardson. We don't know just how honest this guy will be with us. His sister has strongly indicated that there are things in his background that would prove to be very negative should he be arrested."

Wireless was Jacob Greenleaf, the computer genius who Kerry Anderson introduced to Brett and Roger. Jacob was known by the handle "Wireless." Among his many skills, Wireless possessed the ability to enter sites that were otherwise restricted.

"I was thinking the same thing, Brett. We don't have the access that the police have. We can use some x-ray vision and Wireless has access to just about anywhere he chooses to go."

Roger chuckled at his own words and Brett smiled along with him.

"You know, Brett, if Richardson is charged with this crime and you represent him, you'll instantly become the least admired attorney in the state of Florida."

Brett nodded and shrugged.

"Hah, nicely put, my friend. But, as we both know, I've been there before, right about the time when you first met me. In fact, I was least admired nationwide."

Roger laughed.

"Well heck, I liked you from the time that we met... but... of course, I had quite a few beers at the time and, anyway, my endorsement wouldn't carry any weight at all."

Roger laughed. Brett smiled.

"It did with me then and still does," Brett said as he fist-bumped Roger. "Look, I know you're right, Rog. But, if we end up believing the guy is innocent and we refuse to take the case just because of the negative publicity it will generate, then all our big promises about this law practice are nothing more than a sham. We might as well take down the shingle and open up an office cleaning business."

Roger shook his head.

"Uh, uh. That wouldn't sit well with me. I hate the smell of bleach and pine cleaners," Roger said, generating a chuckle from Brett.

∽

Thanks to Wireless, Brett and Roger had insight regarding Chuck Richardson. They learned that Richardson was forty-six, five years younger than his sister, Jocelyn. Chuck was a victim of borderline intellectual functioning, sometimes referred to as BAIQ.

"A person with below average IQ is functional, but mentally impaired," Roger said. "Their IQ, generally, is in the range of 70-85. Richardson's impairment is not as severe as an IQ below 70 but we're talking about someone who is clearly handicapped."

The reason that Wireless was able to find information about Richardson's mental status was because of a past criminal matter. The police arrested Chuck for indecent exposure at the age of fourteen.

"It happened again the next year," Roger said, "and Chuck ended up spending a year in a juvenile detention center."

Then, when Chuck was nineteen, he got a job working in a hospital laundry room.

"Chuck had a reputation for being a good worker," Roger said, "but, after six months of employment, the hospital fired him. Wireless hacked into the hospital administrative files and found three communications from female employees who also worked in the laundry room. All three claimed Chuck made lewd and suggestive remarks causing them to feel uncomfortable around him. The hospital never cited these complaints when they fired Chuck. They didn't want to generate any negative publicity nor place these females in a precarious position."

"The *coup de gras* occurred," Roger said, "when Richardson was twenty-four-years-old. A young girl claimed that Chuck attempted to rape her. Because of his low IQ, the DA opted not to bring Chuck to trial. His attorney worked out a settlement whereby Richardson spent three years in a state mental rehabilitative hospital. Afterwards, the court placed Chuck on probation for three years."

"I assume," Brett said, "that all of Chuck's past indiscretions were expunged."

"Right," Roger answered. "Otherwise, if the school had known about his past, they would never have hired Chuck. In recent times, Chuck has stayed out of trouble. But let's not kid ourselves. If Chuck is accused of murdering a high school girl, there's gonna be some big-time digging into his past. And a guy with mental problems and incidents of a sexual nature—yeah, he's gonna stir a lot of negative reaction. Folks will be out at night carrying torches and searching for a monster like in that Frankenstein book. Let's face it, Brett, Charles Richardson has all the makings of a prime suspect."

"Or," Brett said, "an easy mark to pin a crime like this on."

⌒◯

Jocelyn McCallister had arranged for Brett to meet with Chuck at her home. They sat together in the sun room. Roger spent time with Jocelyn gathering more background info.

Richardson was five feet eight inches tall. His body was burly. Despite extra weight around his stomach, his upper body was well-developed. His curly red hair was short. He often focused his blue eyes somewhere other than on the person with whom he was speaking.

"Mister Richardson, my name is Brett Gatlin. I am an attorney. Your sister, Jocelyn, asked me to come here and speak with you."

"Jocelyn is nice. She makes me food and stuff."

"Chuck, the police have not charged you with doing anything wrong."

"I didn't do bad things," Chuck said. "I've been good, you know? Promised Jocelyn I would. They talk to me about things I know nothing about."

"Okay, Chuck, to preserve anything you say to me, you can consider me your attorney for now. Whatever you say to me remains between us only. Do you understand?"

"Somebody took the girl," Richardson said. "She was from my school, you know? And somebody took her away."

Richardson would either look away or drop his eyes downward when Brett was speaking to him. Brett regarded those mannerisms as signs of Chuck's mental frailties, but he knew others could read them as evidence of dishonesty.

"Chuck, look at me. Listen to me. Did you hurt this girl? Did you do this?"

"I never hurt nobody. Never."

"Did you know Kelly Ann Lauren?"

"I would never hurt nobody."

"Chuck, did you know Kelly Ann?"

"Who's that?"

"Kelly Ann Lauren is the girl that was taken away by someone and found dead."

"Somebody killed her? Why did they do that?"

Gatlin continued to study Richardson as they spoke together. He wondered whether Chuck was capable of exaggerating his mental limitations.

"Chuck, I need you to concentrate. What I am asking you is extremely important. Can you do that?"

Initially, Chuck did not respond. Brett's reference to the need to concentrate only served to increase pressure on Chuck. Brett spotted this and spoke again.

"Hey, Chuck, forget what I just said. I need you to relax. Close your eyes for a moment. Take a few deep breaths. Everything is going to be fine, Chuck."

Chuck did everything that Brett asked him to do and already was calmer.

"You're doing great," Brett said. "We're going to play a little game, Chuck. You keep your eyes closed, I'll ask you questions, and we'll see how many you can answer. Okay?"

"Yeah, okay," Chuck said. "You gonna keep score?"

"Yes, I'll keep score. You just relax and do the best you can. Think you can do that?"

Chuck kept his eyes closed.

"Yes. I'm gonna try to do real good."

"Great. Where were you last night? Were you at the school when the girls were practicing basketball? Were you there, Chuck?"

"They're good, you know. They win games."

"Chuck, I asked you a question. Were you at the school last night?"

"Yeah. Me and Toby was working on that room that flooded. We had to pull stuff out in the hall and then take it away. You can't do that when the kids are in school."

"Toby? Who's Toby?"

"He works with me. Our boss, Nevin, he had us working at night, so we could pull all that wet, messy stuff out in the hall then take it away."

"Do you know Toby's last name, Chuck?"

Chuck did not.

"Did you and Toby leave at the same time?"

"Nevin said me and Toby did a good job."

"I'm sure you did. But, tell me, did you and Toby leave the school at the same time?"

"Well. Toby needed to pick up his wife and his boy."

"Chuck, I'm asking you if you and Toby left the school building at the same time."

"I told Toby I'd stay and pick up tools and stuff."

"Okay, so, Toby left before you did. Is that right, Chuck?"

"I picked up tools and things for the next time we work."

"Chuck, did you see the girls practicing basketball?"

"They're all so pretty wearing their shorts. And, they play good, you know?"

Brett grimaced. If Chuck was not guilty, he had an uncanny ability to say the wrong thing time and again.

"Chuck, last night, both when you were with Toby and when you were alone, did you, at any time, see any of the girls who had come to practice at the gym?"

Chuck sat silently. He furrowed his brow. He began running his hands through his hair and opening his mouth, while saying nothing. At this point, Brett knew that no matter what Chuck's answer would be, taking this long to answer the question would leave others with the impression that Chuck was hiding something.

"No. We never seen no girls last night."

"What did you do after you finished picking up the tools?"

"We got a door at the back of the building. That's where me and Toby park our cars. So, I went out the door and drove home."

Brett stared at Chuck, got him to make eye contact, and asked the question again.

"Chuck, I'm your lawyer. But I can only help you if you're honest with me. I need you to promise to never lie to me. Chuck did you kill this young girl? Did you kill her, Chuck?"

Richardson's eyes filled with tears. He shook his head violently. His hands were trembling.

"No, no, no. I ain't never hurt nobody. Never."

CHAPTER SEVEN

Just a Matter of Time

Roger was driving, traveling west on I-10, when the two men made a decision to stop on the way back home and get something to eat. They sat together at a small diner. Both men ordered coffee and a sandwich.

"As you know, Rog, just because someone is mentally challenged, that doesn't preclude them from the ability to distinguish right from wrong. A prosecutor can establish that with Richardson. One thing I can tell you for sure is that Richardson is a master at blurting out self-incriminating statements."

Roger put his sandwich down, took a drink of his coffee, and looked up at Brett.

"Public reaction on this case is strong. The pressure is on the Tallahassee PD. They're going to want to make an arrest as soon as possible to calm things down."

Brett nodded.

"And Chuck Richardson is a great candidate for that," Brett said.

Roger washed down a bite of his sandwich.

"What are your honest feelings about this guy, Brett?"

Gatlin hesitated before speaking. He was frowning, looking down at the table, and playing with his fork. He lifted his head and made eye contact with Roger.

"I really can't say, Rog. It's one thing when you're talking with someone who has greater comprehension than Richardson. You can take a reading based upon normal human standards and reactions. That's harder to do when it comes to this man. Sometimes, even when he is making sense, he speaks on the level of a juvenile."

Roger nodded and took another sip of his coffee before responding.

"So, if you represent him, you're going to want a professional to evaluate him."

Once again, Brett nodded his head.

"Yeah, that'll help somewhat, but it's not the total answer. We already know the guy is mentally challenged. What we don't know is when Richardson is telling the truth, when he's not, and when he might not be fully capable of knowing whether he's being honest."

"What about his sister, Jocelyn?" Roger said. "I'll bet she can read the guy better than anyone. Any chance we can utilize her to some degree?"

"I've certainly considered that, Rog."

Brett took another bite of his sandwich and sip of his drink.

"I'd like you to meet Chuck, also. Your insights will help."

"Why is that, Brett? Because you consider me to be a bit off-tilt," Roger said, before breaking out into a laugh.

Brett laughed with him.

"Truth is, I may possibly be the one who needs his head examined for getting involved in this case," Brett said.

"Nah," Roger said. "This is clearly a Gatlin case. At this stage of things, we may have a client who is a perfect patsy to be set up by the police."

Brett nodded, took another bite of his sandwich, and followed it with some coffee.

"Exactly, and I'm telling you, Rog, wait until you meet this guy. Once they have him in custody, there's no telling what he'll confess to."

∽

That evening Brett called Tara. His heart was fluttering, his hands were clammy, and he battled against hanging up before the call went through. But once he heard Tara's voice, a flood of joy raced through his body. Tara did not raise any questions about why it took so many days for Brett to call her. She inquired about how things were going on his end, told him about some of the things that she had been working on, and at times laughed along with Brett.

Before the call ended, Tara said, "I miss you Attorney Gatlin. In fact, I missed you the moment we said goodnight after a wonderful evening together."

"I'll do a better job keeping in touch," Brett said. "Keep an eye on the calendar for when we can see each other again."

"I'd love that," Tara said.

"I would, too. Looks like I may be involved in a major case that could tie me up a lot," Brett said, "but somehow, some way, I'll find a time to be with you again."

∽

The chief detective and the district attorney were at a table in a local Tallahassee diner. They were situated where no one else could hear their conversation.

"All I know is he's an attorney out of the Pensacola area. Richardson's sister retained the guy," the detective said.

The DA smirked and pushed back in his chair.

"Remember, Bradley, you're the one with the most to lose," he said. "If you want things to proceed smoothly, keep a close eye on this. We don't need some out-of-town-lawyer coming in and stirring up trouble."

The DA rose from his chair, paused, and pointed at the chief detective.

"You make sure and keep me informed, you hear?"

∽

He positioned himself so that he had a full view of the gymnasium floor, although no one else knew that he was there. The girls had run drills, practiced shooting free throws, and were now scrimmaging against each other. But he was not interested in their techniques and skills. Young girls, wearing shorts, looking good—his skin was already flushed. He was experiencing the sensation of his hair raising on his arms and nape. The shiver that passed through his body was a source of pleasure.

My, my, so many to choose from. This would not be easy for someone who has difficulty focusing at times like this. He smiled and quietly left the gym. He was not in a hurry. He would make his next move when the time was right.

∽

Before he met with Chuck, Brett had asked Jocelyn if it was possible for Chuck to stay at her home to further protect and isolate him.

"Absolutely," Jocelyn said. "After you talk with him, I'll go with him over to his apartment and get him to gather up whatever he needs. We will leave his car at the back of my property where it cannot be seen. I will also drive Chuck to work in the mornings and pick him up when his workday is finished."

Before he left Jocelyn's home, Brett gave Chuck a warning he would repeat many times in the days to come.

"Do not say a word to anyone, not Toby, not your boss, not even Jocelyn. And if the police tell you they want to talk, you give them one of my business cards and tell them you can only talk if your lawyer is there, also. Do you understand that?"

Chuck said that he did. Gatlin would contact officials at the Tallahassee Police Department and the office of District Attorney William Farragut to be sure they knew that he was representing Charles Richardson.

"I'm pleased, very pleased, that you have agreed to represent Chuck," Jocelyn McCallister said. She was on the phone with Gatlin the morning following his visit with her brother. "Please let me know what I need to do to add to our retainer."

"I appreciate that, Jocelyn, but you need to slow down a bit. The police have not arrested Chuck. There are precautions we need to take, but we're in a wait-and-see mode."

Jocelyn never hesitated. Gatlin was aware that the woman was deeply protective of her brother and most certainly biased in his favor. But, the more he was around her, the more Brett realized that Jocelyn McCallister was an astute woman.

"But we both know he will be arrested. It's just a matter of time. You can bet the authorities are working to strengthen a case against Chuck even now. But they won't wait too much longer. They need an arrest to quell the media and the public. And they need one soon. Chuck is already a popular subject of discussion with the media. And we're not hearing of any new suspects or developments in the case. Everyone seems to be waiting for the police to make the arrest. We've had the press gathered outside Chuck's apartment. Since my home is in a gated community, we should be spared from that.

Like I said, I'm going to keep them away from my brother by driving him to work and picking him up at the end of his shift. On a positive note, the school is not permitting anyone from the press to enter the building at any time."

"So far, so good," Gatlin said.

Brett could hear Jocelyn sigh.

"Yeah, but let's be honest here," she said. "We both know that it's only a matter of time. Arresting Chuck would go a long way in taking pressure off the Tallahassee PD."

Gatlin did not respond. Jocelyn was right and he knew it. Chuck, with his tawdry past and unique ability to incriminate himself, was a perfect suspect. Like Jocelyn, Brett believed that the police were focused on Chuck Richardson and doing whatever they could to build a stronger case against the man.

Brett reminded Jocelyn of the need to continue to do all she could to keep her brother under control and keep him from speaking to anyone.

"Appreciate all you're doing, Jocelyn. And I can't help but believe that no one knows how to handle your brother better than you. We need to know where he is at all times and do all we can to keep him from talking about anything to do with this case and the police interest in him. There are enough things about Chuck that can help make the job that the police have easier. Let's not add to the list."

Within the next half hour, things took a significant turn.

⚜

"Attorney Brett Gatlin? I'm Detective Wilson Jones, Violent Crimes Unit, Tallahassee PD. Sir, am I correct that you are the attorney of record for a Mister Charles Richardson?"

"Yes," Brett said. "That is correct."

"Mister Gatlin, I believe you may have been told that we'd like to meet with your client, if he and you are willing to come in to the station. I was wondering if tomorrow morning at, say, 10:00, would work for you."

"Chuck will be working tomorrow, Detective. Can we change that meeting time to 3:30?"

"Yes, Mister Gatlin. That'll be fine."

"Okay, then I'll bring him in right after his work day is over," Brett said. "I assume we're talking about your East Seventh Avenue headquarters?"

"Yes, sir," Detective Jones said. "Just enter the building and we'll be sure that the people up front are aware that you and Mister Richardson are expected."

"Detective, is there anything in particular that has prompted this need for you to want to interrogate my client again?"

Jones hesitated before answering.

"Nothing I can discuss at this time, sir. As you know, we're still working a full-scale investigation of this case. I'm sure I don't have to tell you that Mister Richardson remains a person of interest to us. But, as you know, your willingness to come in tomorrow is completely voluntary. Thank you for your cooperation, Mister Gatlin. See you tomorrow afternoon."

CHAPTER EIGHT

Heating Up

The sun had already set. Brett and Roger were together in Gatlin's office. The day's normal work hours were over. The two men would be leaving following this last discussion of the day. The bond between them seemed to grow stronger day-by-day. In truth, after Roger retired from the Air Force, his life lost its purpose and direction. He drank more, gambled more, and could not even imagine what he wanted to do for the rest of his life.

Roger pulled a couple of cold beers from the office refrigerator and handed one to Brett. He tapped his beer can against Brett's and took a drink before speaking.

"Do you think the police have come up with anything additional on Richardson? Are they ready to make an arrest?"

"Hard to say," Brett said. "Surely, they know most of everything we do about Chuck's past. There are some things that will require the police to obtain a court order to acquire."

"While we simply use Wireless to get that info for us," Roger said.

"And, best I know," Gatlin continued, "Jocelyn has kept her brother away from the media or anyone else he might say anything to."

"Yeah, but Chuck did report back to work today. It's possible he's been talking with a co-worker," Roger said.

Brett nodded his head and shrugged.

"Yeah, that's the one area that has troubled me the most. And getting Richardson to keep his mouth shut is going to be a formidable task."

"We've been expecting the police to make a move against Chuckie Boy from day one," Roger said. "They may be trying to just add a little more to the pot before arresting him."

Brett took another slug from his beer, then finished off the can.

"Well, I guess we're going to know a whole lot more after tomorrow afternoon. What do we know about this Detective Wilson Jones?"

Roger lifted his phone and pulled up the screen where he had added some background notes.

"Well, let's see what we've got here," Roger said. "Wilson Jones was born in Tampa and joined the Tallahassee PD fifteen years ago. The Department promoted him to detective eight years ago. Jones has worked in the VCU, or Violent Crimes Unit, for the past five years. The VCU investigates murders, which is why they have the lead on the Kelly Ann Lauren case. Tallahassee PD has a Special Victims Unit or SVU that investigates crimes against children. The murder of Kelly Ann trumped the SVU and turned the case over to Jones and his team.

Jones is a college grad. He attended Florida State University which first brought him into the Tallahassee area. He graduated *cum laude* with a degree in Criminal Justice. He's African- American. He met his wife, Bianca, in college. They have three children and a Rottweiler dog. Wireless did some preliminary digging and found several commendations that Detective Jones has received. Looks like the guy is a solid police officer with an excellent reputation. Jones' boss is Chief Detective Daniel Bradley who heads up the detective division. Bradley is about two years away from retirement, but word is he may opt out early next year to run for state representative from Leon County's District 9. That could open the door for Wilson Jones to take Bradley's place as chief detective."

Brett had his eyes closed as he listened intently to all that Roger was saying. He was about to ask Roger for a copy of his notes, when Roger spoke again.

"Betty Jo left for the day. She had to bring her daughter to the dentist. But, she's gonna shoot a copy of this background info and some pics to your phone this evening."

Brett nodded.

"You know, Rog, Detective Jones wouldn't tell me why they want to sit with Richardson again, so I have no idea whether an arrest is pending or what they're up to."

"Yeah," Roger said, "and I asked Wireless to see if he could find out whether anyone else is being called in by Tallahassee PD."

Roger gathered up the two empty beer cans and headed towards the breakroom when he stopped, turned, and faced Brett.

"How're things going with Tara?"

Gatlin smiled.

"We talk every night—like two people who've known each other all of our lives. We talk about work, about how the day went, about things we like and don't like. She's incredibly easy and enjoyable to talk with. And it seems we always find things to laugh about."

Roger smiled and flashed a thumbs-up.

~

Michelle Landry was only fifteen years old but could easily pass for eighteen. As a sophomore at Fulbright, she was in her second year as a member of the girl's varsity basketball team. She was also active on the school drama club and science club which had her quite stretched. Her daddy would not be pleased if he learned that her grades were slipping, especially a 'D' in Biology. If he found out, he'd make her quit playing basketball, which would devastate her. Michelle was desperate.

~

On a night when the moon often disappeared behind the clouds, his vehicle was not conspicuous. Besides, no one was watching the Landry home in particular. At this hour of the night, the household was asleep. Doctor Holden Landry had a successful internal medicine practice. His wife, Lisa, spearheaded a number of local charity events, while also bearing the primary parental responsibilities for Michelle and her two younger brothers. Holden and Lisa Landry were pillars in the community. Michelle was well aware of her responsibility to uphold the reputation of her family. That was quite a burden to thrust upon a young girl, but Michelle knew there was really no way out.

∽

He had the car engine, headlights, and interior lights all turned off. He had no intention of doing anything tonight, anyway. In fact, he had not even planned to be here, but the compulsions he dealt with were often too strong for him to resist. He never did understand them. And, if anything, they seemed to be getting stronger and unable to be fully satisfied.

He stared up at the second-floor room that he imagined would be Michelle's bedroom. Hmm, a fifteen-year-old girl in an eighteen-year-old body was right up his alley.

There was time. No need to be careless. He might give others the impression of not being astute, but he was smarter than they might think. A lot smarter. Things were hot right now, but the police could only do so much to protect and investigate. The time for action would come when…

Just that quickly everything changed. He spotted the car as it stopped at the corner some five houses away from her own. She quickly exited and had hardly begun walking when the car made a U-turn and sped away. She started walking rapidly towards her home. Her plan was to use the side door entrance and climb the stairs to her room before anyone ever realized she'd been gone. He never expected this. Never expected this at all. Michelle Landry had not been in her room this entire time. She was outside, somewhere in the night. And now, she was alone, vulnerable, and available.

∽

Chuck Richardson moved quietly through the house to the bedroom his sister had designated for him. He liked it there well enough, although he preferred his own small apartment. The room he was in now had its own restroom—that was cool. It had cathedral ceilings. He liked that, also. And the bed was more comfortable than the one he had at his place. The room itself, just as with Jocelyn's house, was a whole lot fancier, too.

As he laid his head down on the pillow, his mind was racing with a number of thoughts that were confusing to him. It troubled him that sometimes he did not remember things. There were times when he could not explain how he ended up in a certain place or what he had been doing. It was as if he lost track of things and had no memory of them. Chuck never mentioned this to anyone, not even Jocelyn, for fear they'd stick him back in one of those state institutions again where all they do is poke, prod, and subject you to a million tests. He'd had enough of that to last a lifetime. He wondered if all that heavy drinking he did in the past might have done something to screw up his mind. He'd heard somewhere that alcohol can do that, especially when you drink too much like he used to do. He just couldn't remember where he heard that. Maybe, it was in a country song or something.

The police asked him a lot of questions about the girls' basketball team—confusing questions that made him feel uncomfortable. Toby said that's how the police work. They throw a bunch of questions at you to try to get you all confused. Now, they were wanting to talk again tomorrow after work. Well, at least he'd have his lawyer with him. That was a whole lot better. Lawyer Gatlin made him feel protected. You could tell that Gatlin was real smart.

Chuck was having trouble getting to sleep. He shouldn't have left and gone traipsing around in his car like he did. He definitely should not have made that stop. Hopefully, Jocelyn would never know.

CHAPTER NINE

At the Station

Jocelyn picked her brother up at work and brought him home. When Gatlin arrived, Jocelyn was unusually quiet. Her posture was rigid, and she avoided direct eye-contact with Brett.

Richardson, on the other hand, displayed no nervousness or apprehension at all. Gatlin wondered if the man fully comprehended the situation he was in. Chuck was the focus of a homicide investigation that had already sent ripples of fear and anger throughout the city.

"Remember, Chuck, you only answer a question after I tell you to. If I don't want you to answer, I will tell that to the detective, and you are to say nothing at all. Do you understand that, Chuck? Can you do that?"

A big smile covered Richardson's face.

"You mean like 'Simon Says'? You have to ask, 'May I?' before doing anything."

"Okay then, Chuck. You think of that when we're sitting with the detective."

Chuck nodded and acted as if he understood everything that Brett was saying, but Gatlin was unsure that his client genuinely did. Brett was taking a chance in agreeing to permit Chuck to meet again with the police. But he also knew that a refusal to cooperate could cause the police to take other actions. They might issue a subpoena or call a grand jury. They could make the arrest and place Richardson under lawful custody.

Gatlin and Richardson arrived at the Tallahassee Police Headquarters a few minutes prior to 3:30 p.m. A staff member ushered them into a conference room. Thirty-five minutes passed and there was still no sign of Detective Jones. Brett used the time to speak quietly with Chuck. Now, he was questioning just where this detective was. Gatlin and Richardson had voluntarily come to the station. They could leave at any time. Brett stood up. He began to usher Chuck from the room, when the door was thrust open and a man rushed in.

"Gentlemen, forgive me. I apologize for being late. Something urgent came up that I could not avoid. I apologize again. I am Detective Wilson Jones."

The detective stood at six feet two and did not seem to have any excess pounds on his body. His face was warm and friendly. He was dressed in brown slacks, with a light blue dress shirt, and a tan sports coat. His badge was affixed to his pants belt.

Following an offer of coffee and fruit juices, with Gatlin accepting coffee and Chuck opting for apple juice, Jones took the time to prepare to open the interrogation session. He began by informing the parties that everything would be recorded. He cited the names of everyone present, the time, and the location.

"Mister Richardson, you work at the Milford Fulbright High School here in Tallahassee? Is that correct, sir?"

Chuck responded without even considering his attorney.

"Yep, home of the Jaguars. I work there, yep."

"And what is the nature of your employment?"

The fact that Chuck was a bit unsure of the exact meaning of the question slowed him down. Brett stepped in.

"The detective wants to know what kind of work you do at the school, Chuck. That's a question you may answer."

Chuck smiled.

"Me and Toby do all kinds of things. We paint, fix stuff, mop, sweep, and clean things."

"Toby?" Detective Jones said.

Chuck looked towards Gatlin before speaking. Brett nodded his head.

"Yeah, Toby's who I work with."

Brett interrupted.

"My client works with a Toby Parmenter, as part of a light maintenance squad at the school. They receive their work orders from a man named Nevin McGuire. An outside independent contractor crew comes in every evening to do final cleanup work and dispose of the trash. For any major repair needs, McGuire hires someone to come in and handle that on a contract basis."

Brett was sure that Jones would already have acquired a list of all people who work at the school, but he wanted to show a cooperative attitude on behalf of his client.

"Thank you, Counselor," Jones said.

The questions from Detective Jones continued. He was methodical in his approach. "Mister Richardson, did you know Kelly Ann Lauren?"

"Who?" Chuck asked.

"Kelly Ann was the murder victim," the detective said.

"So, she's dead, right?" Chuck said.

"Yes," Jones responded. "Someone killed her."

"Well, I'm sorry somebody did that," Chuck said.

Brett interrupted.

"Chuck, the detective is asking whether you knew Kelly Ann."

"Well, I know somebody took her and she played on the team. Is that knowing her?"

"No," Detective Jones said. "Knowing her would mean you and she would speak together and things like that."

"No, I ain't never spoke to any girl on the team. I just watch 'em practice and play."

Jones asked where Chuck was on the night Kelly Ann was murdered. Gatlin noted that the detective was not particularly adversarial towards Richardson and made an effort to speak slowly and use words that would be much easier for Chuck to comprehend. It was not until the end of the interrogation session that things took an abrupt turn in the line of questioning.

Detective Wilson Jones leaned forward. He tilted his head towards the side. He gazed at Chuck Richardson with focus.

"Mister Richardson, I need you to concentrate now. You've seen the girls practicing basketball at the high school. Is that correct, sir?"

For the first time since they were together, Chuck gave the appearance of being uneasy. The challenge to concentrate generated uncertainty in him. Gatlin immediately noticed the change in Chuck's demeanor.

"Chuck, are you alright?" Gatlin asked. "Do you need a break, a glass of water, or maybe some more apple juice?"

Chuck shook his head. Gatlin continued.

"Chuck, I want you to take a minute and stand up. You can walk over to the wall and back. Just stretch your legs and catch your breath."

Chuck stood up and walked to the wall and back. Then, he sat down again.

"Are we okay now?" Detective Jones asked.

Gatlin looked over at his client, then nodded for Jones to continue. Just then, another man entered the room and sat down next to Jones. The man appeared to be in his late fifties, had thick brown hair, a square jaw, brown eyes, and was somewhere around six feet three inches tall.

"Excuse me, gentlemen," Detective Jones said, "this is Chief Detective Daniel Bradley."

Bradley nodded, but did not speak.

"Okay, as I was saying," Jones said, "you have had opportunity to watch the girls' basketball team practice or play a game. Is that true, Mister Richardson?"

"Yeah, I seen 'em practice at the gym. And one time, I had to fix a few of them gym chairs. It ain't all that hard to do. You just gotta unscrew and take the old seat off, then you put the new one on. I was good at it, so Nevin had me do it. Toby was still workin' … uh … someplace else. I don't remember."

"And the girls were in there practicing?" Detective Jones said.

"Yeah, they was practicing. They're good, you know? They win lots of games."

"Did you enjoy watching them?"

Brett's body stiffened. He stared intensely at his client and prepared to stop Chuck from speaking based upon where this line of questioning might lead to. He was relieved that Chuck's succinct answer contained none of his usual comments about how good the girls look in shorts.

"I like watching them."

"Mister Richardson," Detective Wilson said, "have you ever seen the girls play a game. I'm talking about a game against another school.

Chuck smiled.

"Me and Jocelyn ... "

"My client is referring to Miss Jocelyn McCallister, a resident of Tallahassee and, I would assume you know, his sister," Gatlin said.

"Thank you, Counselor" Jones said. "Please continue, Mister Richardson."

Chuck did not immediately recall what he was saying when his attorney interrupted.

"Chuck, Detective Jones asked you whether you've ever seen the Fulbright High School girls' basketball team play a game. You mentioned that you have seen them practice in a gym and that at you and Jocelyn ... "

"Yeah, oh yeah, me and Jocelyn, we went to see a game the girls played one night at the school. They played good, you know? They won."

"Do you remember who they played in that game?" Jones asked.

Chuck furrowed his brow and then closed his eyes. He opened them and spoke again.

Vincent J. Sachar

"They had blue uniforms. Our girls wear red. That's all I remember. And our girls were the pretty ones. Better looking, you know?"

"You like looking at our girls? You think they look pretty, even sexy in their uniforms?" Wilson Jones said.

"We're going to object to that question," Gatlin said, "and I don't want you to answer that, Chuck."

Jones paused, sighed deeply, then leaned forward, placing his face closer to Richardson than ever before.

"Mister Richardson, do you know who Michelle Landry is? Do you know her?"

Chuck said nothing.

"Are you referring to a member of the Fulbright High girls' basketball team?" Gatlin said.

"I am," Jones said. "I am referring to a fifteen-year-old student who is on the team. Yes, I want to know if your client knows Michelle Landry."

"You may answer the question, Chuck," Gatlin said.

"I seen the girls sometimes. They play real good. I like watching 'em play."

"Chuck," Brett Gatlin interrupted, "do you know these girls or any of them by name? Do you ever talk to them yourself?"

Chuck paused.

"N-no, I don't know 'em. I don't never talk with 'em. I just seen 'em practice and went to a game with Jocelyn. And, they play real good, you know?"

"So, you do not know who Michelle Landry is?" Jones asked.

"Maybe I seen her practicing or something if she plays on the team."

"I'll take that as a 'no,' " Jones said.

"Why are you asking about a girl named Landry?" Brett said.

"She's been reported as missing," Detective Jones said. "We have not yet determined whether she ran away or has been abducted. All we know is her parents believed she was asleep in her bedroom last night, but, as of this morning, there's no sign of her."

Jones turned towards Chuck.

"I need to ask you, Mister Richardson, where you were last night?"

Chuck turned towards Brett Gatlin as if he just remembered that he was supposed to ask, 'May I?' before answering questions from the detective. Brett smiled.

"Chuck, please feel free to answer the detective's question."

"I stay at Jocelyn's. That's where I sleep, you know? And she brings me to work and picks me up when I'm finished."

"That'd be the aforementioned sister, Jocelyn McCallister?" Jones said.

"Yes, I asked Miss McCallister to permit her brother to stay with her during this time when he is ... " Brett paused and smiled at the detective, "at the very least, a person of interest to Tallahassee PD. If you do not have it, I will provide you with that address, Detective. And, of course, Miss McCallister can verify my client's statement regarding his presence last night."

Detective Wilson Jones thanked Brett Gatlin and Chuck Richardson for their willingness to come into the police station.

Brett shook hands with Detective Wilson Jones. Chief Detective Bradley turned and exited the room without acknowledging Brett.

As they drove back towards Jocelyn's home, Brett had mixed feelings. The possibility that another young girl had been abducted left Brett with a sick feeling. Dear God, he did not want that to be true. But, if it was true, the fact that his client had a verifiable alibi would go a long way to take the focus off of him.

CHAPTER TEN

It Happened Again

After dropping Chuck off at his sister's home, Brett headed back towards his office in Milton. On the way, he called Tara.

"Yeah, I'm headed back now. Roger and I are going to have dinner together and use the time to update each other. If it's okay with you. I'll call you when I get back home."

"Of course, it's okay," Tara said, "provided you know that I never want you to feel pressured about calling me when you're involved in so much. Just know that I understand and also know that I absolutely love it whenever I hear your voice."

⁂

Roger was at the office when Brett arrived. He intercepted Brett as he entered the building, ushered him into his office, and quickly shut the door. Brett sat in a chair opposite Roger's desk. Roger sat on the desk.

"Okay, Bubba," Roger said, "before we head out to get a bite to eat, we need to take a few minutes and talk. Man, I hate to steal your thunder, but a lot of what you were going to tell me is already old news. I know about the missing Landry girl. The police have no updates on this yet. Did she run away from home? Was she abducted? They still don't know. What we do know is that the police are convinced that she left her home on her own last night."

"Sounds like you've been getting info from a hidden unknown source," Brett said.

Roger nodded his head and chuckled.

"Which means this next bit of insight I'm gonna lay on you is something you and I will need to tuck away and act like we don't know a thing about it. Let's just say it's coming from the wrong side of the street."

It was Brett's turn to laugh.

"Sounds to me like someone's been peeking through keyholes into areas that we're barred from," Brett said.

"I'll tell you, man," Roger said, "we best never forget how fortunate we are that Wireless is on our side and not someone we have to contend with. And, we better never cross this dude." Roger chuckled after saying this. "I like Wireless, but the guy's skills are downright spooky."

Roger took a deep breath. He reached over onto the desk and picked up a pen. He began twirling it in his hands.

"Tallahassee PD picked up a guy within the past hour. His name is Edison Peters. Wireless didn't have much to work with so far. From what we do know, Peters lives at a local YMCA. He drives an old beat-up car. He's thirty-eight-years-old, unemployed, has a rap sheet, but we're primarily talking about misdemeanor theft crimes and marijuana possession.

The guy is new in town. A number of witnesses claim they've seen Peters hanging around the high school. That's all we know."

"That's not a lot to go on," Gatlin said.

"Well, there's one more piece to this puzzle," Roger said. "Day before yesterday, Michelle Landry was walking towards the park after school to meet up with a friend. Seems that Peters pulled up in his car and offered a ride to her. Couple of others girls remembered seeing him continuing to follow her, driving slowly, trying to coax her to get in the car. She never did."

Both Brett and Roger realized that none of this provided any assurance that Edison Peters had anything to do with Michelle Landry's disappearance. Besides, the police still did not know whether Landry had, in fact, been abducted. But there was a link. Tallahassee PD would follow up on this. And, the good news was that none of this had anything to do with Chuck Richardson.

⁂

There are times when a certain news story grips the very heart and soul of a city. It requires no added sensationalism or embellishments. It moves at a pace beyond the incredible power and speed of the media, as if it has a life and force of its own. People who do not even watch the news on television or pick up a newspaper, nevertheless, somehow know about it.

Waves of shock and fear rippled throughout the community at the news that evening that the body of Michelle Landry had been found in a wooded area located two miles from the Landry home. The police were not releasing a great deal of information regarding the cause of death and whether she had been sexually assaulted. To the public, none of those details were all that important. What mattered was that another young girl's life had been cut short, cheating her of all the things that girls her age dream of experiencing. What also was a primary matter of concern was the fact that young girls throughout the community were still at risk.

The media was already talking about a serial killer. Many parents were seeking alternatives to sending their daughters to school. Inquiries into homeschooling requirements in Florida were off the charts.

A wave of fear was sweeping throughout the city. The Tallahassee Police Department was battling against the incredible pressure that every young girl in the city was in danger until the person responsible for these hideous acts was in custody.

Roger and Brett had dinner together then headed their separate ways. When the news about Michelle broke, Roger was at his condo. He called Brett.

"Yeah, I've been watching the news reports on television," Brett said. "I was afraid when we first heard about the Landry girl that it was going to come to this."

"Not me," Roger said. "I guess I was lying to myself. I was doing everything to believe that the murder of Kelly Ann Lauren was an isolated incident. I had already convinced myself that Michelle Landry had run away from home. I wasn't prepared for this."

"Let's face it, Rog, there's no way we can understand how or why someone would do a thing like this. Now, we have to hope that the police will quickly find who's behind it."

"What about Chuck Richardson, Brett? Does tonight's news change things for him?"

"We're going to have to see what the medical examiner comes up with on a time of death," Brett said, "but, assuming we're talking about last night, our client has a solid alibi. Detective Wilson Jones was going to follow up with Jocelyn to confirm it. Not sure if he's done so, yet. He might not have since, before now, the issue of whether Michelle had run away from home had not yet been resolved. But, there's no problem either way. Chuck was at the home of his sister throughout the night. Jocelyn told me when she took her brother in that she changed the password of the house alarm without telling Chuck. He would not be able to leave that home without triggering the alarm."

↝

"Oh, Brett, another victim. It's all over the news. Such a terrible tragedy."

Tara was on the phone with Brett. The discussion they were having was about the murders of young girls occurring in the Tallahassee area on the very case that Gatlin was involved in.

"It's horrendous, Tara. My client has a solid alibi, but we're still talking about a monster out there somewhere who has the entire community in a panic."

"This has to be extremely troubling for you," Tara said. "Are you okay? I'm worried about you, Brett. I know you were highly-trained and dealt with a great deal of pressure as a federal agent but... "

"No, you're right, Tara. This is different. We're not talking about drug cartels and dealers. We're dealing with young innocent girls and I have a client who, regardless of a current air-tight alibi, is sure to still be of interest to the police."

"Please be careful, Darling," Tara said. "And know that I'm here. You can call me any time day or night. I may not be able to help you resolve things, but I've got a listening ear and a... a loving heart."

Brett thanked Tara, promised to call again soon, and told her how much he appreciated having her in his life.

Appreciated? What kind of comment was that? Why didn't he tell her that he was falling in love with her? He never told that to Kerry. Now, he was doing the same thing with Tara.

I spent too many years working in an environment where I could never trust anyone. My heart was ruled by cynicism and a refusal to ever let my guard down. But I'm no longer working undercover with a false ID. I'm not a fugitive running from the law. I based my unwillingness to express my feelings to Kerry on the circumstances we were under. I was being charged with treason and murder and Kerry was a national reporter defending me. Now, I'm seeing that my reluctance to express my feelings may have been something inside of me.

✍

He was seated in a chair in the bedroom. He had never drunk Black Jack Daniels straight from the bottle as he was doing now. But he had never been in the position that he was now. He had no control over his rasping breaths and full body tremors. He tried, desperately tried, to regain control of his mind and body, but his explosive emotions and the effect of the whiskey were hurdles he could not overcome.

Until now, he was convinced that no one would ever suspect any link between him and the Landry girl. But now, the police would be looking closer at everything and anything involving Michelle. His body was shaking so uncontrollably that he considered he might be on the verge of suffering a heart attack. He also considered that might be the best way out for him.

They will find out. They're gonna know. They always know. They're smart, smarter than me. I'm dead. I'm finished. It doesn't matter what I do. It's over. No way out.

He thought of the .38 Chief's Special that he had hidden away in the closet when he first came to this room. No one knew that he had it. He opened the closet door and retrieved the weapon. He didn't even know much about the gun at all, except that it was loaded. He sat at the edge of the bed and pressed the barrel of the gun against his temple. His hand continued to shake making it difficult to keep the gun in place.

But, no matter how hard he tried to pull the trigger, he just could not do it. He tried several times and each time ended up pulling the gun away. Finally, he let the weapon fall to the floor, threw himself across the bed, and sobbed.

CHAPTER ELEVEN

Losing the Safeguard

It took a moment or two for Brett's mind to grasp that the annoying sound disrupting his sleep at 6:15 a.m. was his cell phone signaling that a call was coming through. He answered with a quick "Hello." His raspy voice evidenced that was the first word he had spoken on this day.

"I'm sorry for calling this early. Forgive me. I wouldn't have if it were not an emergency."

The caller paused for a moment before identifying herself as Jocelyn McCallister. By then, Brett had recognized her voice.

"We need to talk. I need you. Please. I don't know what to do and they're going to come here. You know they will. I need help. If … if this is beyond the scope of your representation of Chuck, I'll pay you something additional. You've got to talk with me before they … "

"Whoa, slow down, Jocelyn. Stop for a moment. Take a deep breath and tell me what in the world you're talking about."

Jocelyn did slow down. Brett could hear her breathing deeply. When she began to speak again, her voice was still tight and edgy, but she was making a concerted effort to communicate on a calmer basis.

"Now, a second victim has been discovered. The police are going to come here again. Who knows? Talk to me. Try to talk to Chuck again. You know they will. You even said that Detective Wilson, I believe his name is, will want to see me. Before anyone comes here, I need to talk with you. I don't want to do it over the phone. Please, I know it's a burden, but, please, will you come see me?"

Brett agreed that he would. The moment he disconnected from the call, he rose from the bed and headed towards the shower. Afterwards, he'd take an English Muffin and a cup of black coffee with him as he headed towards Tallahassee.

Rather than call Roger and interrupt his Saturday morning sleep, Brett sent a text to let him know what he was up to.

∽

"I ain't had nothing to do with what happened to that girl. And you ain't gonna pin nothing on me."

Hours of questioning throughout the night had taken its toll on Edison Peters. He was beyond tired.

"You keep asking the same stuff and I keep giving you the same answers. I'm telling you. I ain't had nothing to do with that girl's death. You're wasting your time and mine."

Detective Wilson Jones lifted his head when someone came into the room with two cups of coffee. He placed one across the table in front of Peters, along with some creamer, sugar, and a plastic spoon.

"Okay, let's calm down, Mister Peters. Help me, one more time, to be sure I've got my facts straight. Work with me so's I can take your name off my list and move on."

Edison Peters poured two packages of creamer, three packets of sugar, and was stirring his coffee. He focused his eyes on the Styrofoam cup and watched the caramel-colored liquid spin a circle before he took his first sip.

"We have already verified that you made an attempt to engage with Miss Michelle Landry outside Fulbright High the day before she disappeared."

Peters' hand was shaking as he carefully took his first sip of the hot brew.

"I seen a pretty young lady. Looked like she was old enough for me to approach. I'm new in town. Don't know nobody. Ain't nothing wrong with a man exploring the possibility of meeting a female for a little companionship, is there?"

Wilson finished his sip of coffee and placed the cup back down on the table. He had waited hours before bringing up this next point. He wanted to catch Edison Peters at a time when the man was particularly vulnerable. Wilson believed that time had now come.

"Okay, for the moment, Peters, I'm going to disregard the fact that Michelle Landry appeared older than she actually was and move past that point. We have a witness who believes he saw a vehicle matching yours outside the Landry house on the night Michelle disappeared. Was that you? And, if so, how did you find out the young lady's name and where she lived? What were you doing there on the very night when Michelle Landry disappeared?"

Peters bolted upright. His face was red. He glared at the detective. He curled his hands into fists. His abrupt movements caused his cup of coffee to fall from the table and spill out onto the floor.

"That's a lie. I'm being set up. You trying to make me your patsy."

"Sit down—now, Peters."

Wilson was on his feet, also. The ruckus caused another one of the detectives, who had been observing the session through a two-way mirror, to enter the room. But Wilson lifted his hand with his palm facing towards his colleague to indicate that things were not out-of-control. Peters was back in his seat.

"Ain't nobody gonna play me for a fool," Edison Peters said. "Nobody. I know my rights. I want a lawyer. I ain't got nothing more to say."

∽

The house was quiet when Gatlin arrived. Jocelyn had some fresh coffee brewed and a platter of pastries. She directed Brett to sit with her in the sunroom. Brett opted for coffee, only.

"Where's Chuck now?" Brett asked.

"He's still asleep in his room. I've not heard anything from him so far this morning."

Brett noted the tightness in Jocelyn's face and the slight trembling in her hands.

"Okay, tell me what's on your mind, Jocelyn. What has you so stirred up? The death of Michelle Landry is horrific and has everyone on edge. But what has caused you to react as you have this morning?"

Jocelyn continued to rub her arms, as if she were cold, and look around the room. Then, before she spoke, she began to bounce a curled knuckle against her front teeth. Her breathing was accelerated, and she rocked in her seat.

"I-I thought I had everything under control. I really did. I had him sleeping here just like you asked me to do. I drove Chuck to work and picked him up at the end of the day. I changed the security system password and never told Chuck I had done so. I had Chuck park his car behind the house. I did everything I knew to do to make sure I had things secure. I don't know what more I could have done."

Jocelyn stopped speaking. Her lips trembled.

"I-I d-don't k-know what happened. I can't figure out how. I mean, I thought… "

Brett reached over and placed his hand on Jocelyn's arm. She sighed deeply. Her head was down as she continued to speak.

"On the night th-that the Landry girl disappeared… as best I knew, Chuck was here in the house all night. But, later… later that next morning, I-I went out back to water a few plants. Th-that's when I noticed it. Made no sense at first."

Jocelyn lifted her head and made direct eye contact with Gatlin.

"Chuck's car—it had been moved during the night."

Brett's mouth fell open. A tingling feeling throughout his body accompanied the flush of adrenaline as his mind raced to put together the meaning of all that he was now hearing.

"At first, I tried to convince myself that I was mistaken. But I knew I wasn't. There was no question in my mind."

Jocelyn reached over to a box of tissues and softly dabbed her eyes.

"I've racked my brain trying to figure out how Chuck could have discovered the changed security system password. Best I could determine, I did find a small slip of paper in the kitchen where I originally wrote down the new four-digit code. That's the thing with Chuck. With his limited abilities, it's so difficult to gauge just what he's capable of doing or figuring out. Sometimes, he'll do something that you would think was beyond his capabilities. Other times, he struggles comprehending something quite simple. He has surprised me many times in the past."

Brett spoke calmly in an effort to keep Jocelyn from being any more upset than she already was.

"You've not said anything to Chuck about this?"

"Not a word. I was so shocked by what I was seeing and, to be honest with you, I was scared and ashamed."

"Ashamed? I'm not grasping that, Jocelyn."

Tears began to flow from Jocelyn's eyes.

"I told you that I would take charge of my brother, help protect him during a vulnerable time in his life. I wanted to provide a safeguard for Chuck. I wanted to assist you in your job. I failed in both. That's why I didn't tell you about this right away after I discovered it. Also, I had no idea at the time how important it would be."

Jocelyn stood up, walked over towards the floor-to-ceiling windows that overlooked the backyard, and stared out. She spoke without turning around to face Gatlin.

"He's going to come to me, isn't he? That detective, Wilson Jones. Just like you said he would. He'll ask me to verify

Chuck's alibi on the night that the poor Landry girl went missing."

Jocelyn turned back from the windows. She raised both arms, extended them out, and placed the palms of her hands facing towards Gatlin.

"What do I do now? Do I stick with the story that Chuck was here in this house without ever leaving the entire night? Is that what I do? And if I do that, am I committing a crime of some sort? Or do I put my brother even more at risk by admitting that he may have left this house that night— sometime on the very night when another innocent young girl was murdered?"

"You are not required to volunteer any information to the police, Jocelyn. But, if they ask you a direct question and you lie to generate a solid alibi for your brother, you are subjecting yourself to be charged with obstructing justice."

Jocelyn shivered. She wrapped her own arms around herself and shivered.

"You were right to contact me. We need to speak with Chuck before the police arrive. It's time to find out whether Chuck did drive away and, if so, where he went and what he did."

Until last night, Chuck Richardson appeared to have an airtight alibi. Now, he may have shattered that alibi and made himself vulnerable and exposed to charges of first-degree murder. Chuck had once again raised the question as to whether he did have something to do with the murder of these girls.

CHAPTER TWELVE

What Really Happened

Brett called Roger to tell him what he had just learned and keep him updated.

"I haven't talked with Chuck yet," Brett said, "but wanted you to be aware of this as soon as possible."

"Well, there's no question that it certainly changes things," Roger said. "It doesn't make Chuck a murderer, but it definitely will make it easier for the men in blue to tighten their focus on our boy."

"Yeah," Brett said. "I thought we had an airtight alibi that would, if anything, make everything go away for Chuck. This was the last thing I expected."

"Brett, we're working on the assumption that Chuck is innocent. Does this challenge that position in your mind?"

Brett did not answer right away. That was the key question that first bombarded his mind when he learned that Chuck had somehow discovered how to sneak out of Jocelyn's house during the night.

"I'm still believing that Chuck is neither guilty of nor even capable of murder, but this shakes my belief a bit. Jocelyn said that sometimes Chuck does things that seem to be beyond his mental capacity. It just makes you wonder what this guy is able to do."

Roger paused to gather his thoughts. He remembered how easy it was for everyone to condemn and convict Brett at the time when he first met him. He and Brett didn't know for sure whether Chuck was innocent, although they believed him to be. But Roger knew how easy it would be for the police and the district attorney to lock in on Chuck Richardson as their man. Beyond that, Roger's concern was not limited to Chuck Richardson. He was focused upon Brett and his vulnerabilities in dealing with situations that might conjure up his own past hurts.

"Brett, I'm coming in to Tallahassee. Quick shower and I'm on my way. I've got a few things I want to check into. It wouldn't hurt for us to be a bit proactive, just in case our friends at Tallahassee PD get lazy and start acting like they've got no further searching to do. I know you'll be talking with Chuck and trying to get a better handle on what in the world that guy's been up to. Just know that I'll be there in the State Capital if you need me."

⁂

Jocelyn knocked on Chuck's bedroom door and called out his name. When she received a response, she spoke loud and slowly to convey the message she wanted her brother to hear.

"Chuck, your lawyer, Attorney Gatlin, is here. We need you to come out and sit with us."

Every bedroom in Jocelyn's house had its own bathroom with a tub and shower. Chuck did not take the time to shower, but he did wash his face, brush his teeth, and run a brush through his hair.

Jocelyn kept the meeting in the sun room, but made sure that there was coffee, pastries, and some toasted English Muffins with jam for Chuck. Brett wanted Jocelyn to be in the room when he asked Chuck about whether he had ever left the house during the night. In a sense, he believed it was only right that she should be. The police would call upon Jocelyn to verify Chuck's alibi.

When Chuck came out of the room, he was smiling, extended his hand to Brett and hugged his sister. When he did, Jocelyn turned away, touched her throat, and felt a sudden coldness strike at the very core of her being. She made an attempt to regroup and say nothing. The latent smell of alcohol was still on Chuck's breath.

✍

Roger had been unable to shake a pressing thought that arose when he first heard Wireless' account of Edison Peters. The man approached Michelle Landry at a time when she was walking alone to nearby Bryant Park after school had ended for the day. It might mean nothing at all, but Roger wondered why Michelle was headed to a nearby park, rather than leaving the area. He reasoned that she could be going there to meet up with a boy. He asked Wireless to take a closer look at the park Michelle was headed to.

"Bryant Park has a bad rep," Wireless reported back. "There've been a number of drug arrests there—not just drug use, but drug deals. Leads me to believe it's a place where people meet with a drug dealer and get their stuff."

Roger's mind was overloaded with a multitude of thoughts and questions.

Was Michelle Landry using drugs? What happened to Michelle on the night she was killed? There was no way that someone would have snuck into the Landry home, found Michelle asleep in her bedroom, then abducted her without anyone hearing a sound. Besides, that would be much too risky a thing to do. The girl had to have snuck out of the house on her own. Why would she do that? Did someone help her? Where did she go? Two strong motivations causing her to leave her house come to mind. Was she meeting with a boy? Was she going somewhere to do drugs?

Then, Roger took one more step. He asked Wireless to search for anyone who had been arrested for possession of or dealing drugs but was not currently in prison. The list was much too long to be of any use, until Wireless pulled up a name that generated a great deal of interest in Roger.

"The dude's name is Medford Smith," Wireless said, "but here's the link that'll make you want to know more. He was a student at Fulbright High who got caught with drugs and expelled. From what I can see, Smith is twenty-two-years-old and has an apartment close to Fulbright. I have no way of knowing from anything I'm pulling online if our boy, Medford, stays linked to his *alma mater.*"

"This is good stuff, my man," Roger said. "Gives me something to start with. Until now, we've been sitting on the sidelines letting everyone else make the moves. As I mentioned to Brett, it's time now for us to do some hustling and see what we can stir up."

"I'm here if you need me, Roger. Meanwhile, I'll stay eyes-on to anything else we see Tallahassee PD doing."

∽

"Chuck," Brett said, "we need to talk and, more than anything else, I need you to be honest with me. I can't protect you if you're not upfront with me. And, I'm telling you now, the police will know when you're not telling the truth. Lie and you'll be digging some holes so deep you may never get out of them."

Chuck sat across from Brett. He did not make eye contact with him. Brett reached over and gently squeezed Chuck's arm in an effort to get Chuck's attention.

"Chuck, we need to know if you have ever left this house during the night."

Chuck kept his head down and made no response to Brett's question.

"Listen to me, Chuck," Gatlin said, "the police are going to ask this same question. You heard Detective Jones mention that another high school girl may have been abducted—that means taken away by someone. She was murdered, Chuck. If you never left this house, then we are assured that the police cannot accuse you. So, we have to know. You need to be completely honest with us. Two nights ago, Michelle Landry was murdered at night. Did you leave the house that night? Did you leave last night?"

Again, Chuck kept his head down and did not react at all.

Jocelyn bolted upright from her chair. Her face was flushed, her eyes glowered at Chuck. She slammed her fist on the table causing a coffee cup to tumble onto the ceramic tile floor and shatter. As she moved closer to her brother, she stuck her arm out and pointed her finger at his face.

"Chuck, answer your attorney. Answer him now. This is serious."

Tears flowed from Jocelyn's eyes. Chuck did not respond. Brett stood up. He reached out, turned Jocelyn so she was facing him, and spoke to her. His voice was firm, but gentle.

"Please, Jocelyn, I need you to calm down. I know you're upset. I know it's frustrating, but it's up to Chuck whether he wants us to help him or not."

Jocelyn sat, buried her head in her hands, and sobbed.

Chuck lifted his head and stared at his sister. His mouth fell open and his eyes began to water. He began to bite his bottom lip, wrap his arms around his body, and rock in place.

"Don't … don't cry, Jocelyn. Don't cry. I-I'll talk, okay? I didn't want you to know. I didn't mean to do a bad thing."

Jocelyn walked over to Chuck and hugged him.

"Oh, Chuck, just be honest with us. Let us help you. You know I love you."

Chuck was nodding his head. He was focused upon his sister as she sat back down.

Brett leaned forward and called over to Chuck.

"Did you drive away from this house on any night since you've been staying here?"

Chuck was jittery and unable to remain still. With his head facing down, he mumbled and garbled his words as if he were speaking only to himself.

A Presumption of Guilt

"Couldn't sleep no how. Everything was jumping around in my head. Everybody says I did bad things. They keep talking to me about things I never done. They gonna take me away and lock me up just like they done last time. They hurt me when I was in there. I don't wanna ever go there again. Never. I don't want them to lock me up and hurt me again."

"Listen to me," Brett said. "That's exactly what we're trying to make sure doesn't happen, but you need to help us, Chuck."

Chuck lifted his head and made eye contact with Gatlin.

"I'm going to ask you again," Brett said. "Were you out anywhere last night?"

Richardson stared, furrowed his brow, shifted his eyes upwards and to the left as one attempting to recall before answering the question.

"No, no, I was in my room. No. I didn't go nowhere."

"Good. Okay. Now think again. Did you leave and go anywhere the night before last?"

Chuck's eyes were wild, shifting from one thing to another.

"I been sleeping. Then, I woked up. I had bad dreams. I went in the kitchen to get some juice. That's when I saw them numbers on a paper in the kitchen. I figured they was for the alarm. I figured if I drove around a bit, I'd feel better."

"So," Gatlin said, "you left the house and drove away? Where did you go, Chuck? Tell me everywhere you drove to that night, everything you did."

Once again, Chuck dropped his head, stiffened his body, and said nothing.

CHAPTER THIRTEEN

Stalked

Tara was not someone who was easily spooked, but this was different. She never before had a sense that she was possibly being followed or stalked. Initially, she did not think all that much about it, but now it was beginning to creep her out.

She first spotted him outside her apartment building when she returned home from work two days ago. He never spoke to her, but he gestured in such a way that she felt as if he wanted her to know that she was reason for his presence. Then, she spotted him again when she stepped out for lunch with a coworker yesterday. This time he was outside her office building and he followed the two women to a nearby diner where they had lunch. He never entered the diner and was gone when she stepped out afterwards.

Last night, he was there again outside her apartment building when she returned from work. In each instance, he never said a word to her, did not approach her or make direct contact with her in any manner. But he was there again. And now, she was increasingly uncomfortable.

The man never did anything to justify her need to contact the police. Tara chose not to mention anything to Brett. He was dealing with so much at present. She did not want to burden him with something that might be nothing more than an overactive imagination on her part.

But she did not honestly believe that.

⌀

Roger booked a room in a one-level family-owned motel where he could park his Jeep directly outside the door. He texted the name of the motel to Brett and to Betty Jo.

Afterwards, he went into Bryant Park, located near Fulbright High, under the guise that he was looking to buy drugs. He hoped that he would encounter Medford Smith. Instead, he ran into a skinny, haggard young man who was clearly feeling no pain. The emaciated youth was sitting on the ground leaning against a tree. It appeared as if he had not washed nor even brushed his blonde curly hair in quite some time. His facial hair was in need of a trim. His clothes were dirty and worn. His eyes were closed when Roger first approached him, but, as Roger drew near, the young man opened his eyes and smiled.

"'Beauty is truth, truth beauty—that is all ye know on earth, and all ye need to know,'" the young man said, quoting from the poet John Keats' *Ode to a Grecian Urn*. His smile remained, even when his eyes intermittently closed.

"Ah, a lover of the arts and the fine works of the English Romantic poet, Keats," Roger said. "Tell me, friend, how do I find a dispenser of the means to feel as good as you do now."

The young man broadened his smile. "'Death is the veil which those who live call life; They sleep, and it is lifted.'"

Roger stood directly over the young man, shrugged, and shook his head.

"I'm afraid you got me on that one."

"*Prometheus Unbound*—Percy Bysshe Shelley," the young man said. "Was there a finer Romantic Poet?"

"Well said, young man, but you did not answer my question. Perhaps you can tell me where I might find Medford Smith?"

The young man spoke while keeping his eyes shut. His words were slow and slurred as if he were speaking from out of a dream.

"There are those who dwell on West Siemens Avenue. They rule over that land as a lord over his fiefdom in days of old. They supply those who dispense to lowly serfs, like me. If you want that which will bring you peace and composure, you'll have to arrange that by going directly to his source or simply hoping that fate brings you and Smith together at the same time."

The young man faded away into what appeared to be a deep sleep, but, despite the young English Literature wizard's drug-induced state, Roger now had something additional to work with. Medford Smith had a supplier from an area around West Siemens Avenue. Roger used his cell phone and searched for that street name. It popped up instantly confirming that such a place existed within the city limits of Tallahassee. That, in no way, told Roger all that he needed to know, but it was a start. He hoped that Wireless could help fill in the blanks.

⁂

Despite his assurance to his sister that he would cooperate with Brett Gatlin, Chuck's responses to Brett's questions were painstakingly slow in coming. Brett and Jocelyn did learn that Chuck left the house on the night that Michelle Landry was murdered. He stopped at an all-night liquor store where he purchased alcohol for the first time in several years.

"I knowed it was wrong. I ain't had nothing to drink in a long time. I done real good staying away from the stuff," Chuck said. "I was thinking maybe it would help me to relax, slow my crazy thinking down, and get me some sleep. I'm ashamed I done it."

Chuck turned directly towards Brett, avoiding eye contact with Jocelyn.

"I didn't want to hurt Jocelyn. She been so good to me, you know?"

Jocelyn's face was pale. Her lips trembled, but she did her very best to constrain herself and permit Brett to take charge of the situation. She was astute enough to know that the issue was not simply that her brother had gone off the proverbial wagon. Rather, Chuck lost his alibi for the night another young lady was murdered."

"Chuck," Brett said, "I need you to tell me if you had any contact with Michelle Landry that night. Did you go anywhere near her home?"

Chuck tilted his head to the side and pursed his lips. His eyes blinked rapidly. His mouth was open, but nothing came out. After an inordinately long pause, he spoke again.

"How can I know? I drank some liquor and drived around. I don't always remember things. But I don't know no girl by that name. And I didn't go to nobody's house."

Jocelyn grimaced and moaned softly. Brett turned towards her and gently rubbed her hand. He knew that Jocelyn was astute enough to realize that not only did her brother forfeit his solid alibi by leaving the house on that fateful night, his testimony would only make matters worse. Brett's only choice now was to keep Chuck from saying anything to the police, which he could effectively do as the man's attorney, even if Chuck was formally arrested. What Brett could not do was ask Jocelyn to lie to the police. She did not have to provide the details of all that she knew to the authorities. Rather, she would provide an answer that indicated she could not completely guarantee that her brother never left the house at any time during the night.

Brett reached across the table and placed his hand on Chuck's shoulder.

"Chuck, I want you to forget about the liquor you bought and the fact that you snuck away at night. You still have some alcohol left in your room and drank some more last night, didn't you? I'd like you to give it to me. I'd also like you to give me your car keys. You made a mistake, but we all make mistakes sometimes. Are you hearing me, Chuck?"

Chuck nodded. He was genuinely sorry, primarily from knowing he had disappointed his sister more than anything else.

"Yeah," he said. "I don't want to do bad things and I don't want to make Jocelyn sad and cry. I don't want her to be sorry she helps me."

Jocelyn stood up, walked over to Chuck, and hugged him.

"Chuck I'll never be sorry when I help you. I love you and will always be here for you."

"Chuck," Gatlin said, "I don't want you talking to anyone. Not a word to the police or anyone else other than me. Do you understand that?"

"Yeah," Chuck said. "Don't talk to nobody, except my lawyer."

"That's right, Chuck," Brett said. "Simon says you don't talk, you don't say anything to anyone other than me, your lawyer. You got that?"

"Yeah," Chuck said. "Simon says I don't talk."

Brett patted Chuck on his shoulder.

"Remember, if you don't want them to lock you up again, you have to do what I say. And if they do lock you up for a little while, you say nothing and know that Jocelyn and I are going to be working hard to get you free again. Okay, Chuck?"

"Okay," Chuck said. "Simon says I don't talk."

∽

"Siemens Avenue is in a notoriously bad section of town," Wireless said, as he and Roger spoke by phone. "Even the cops are not fond of patrolling in that area. There's a gang named the *West Siemens Gang* who claim that area as their territory. The word is they are one of the primary sources for illegal street drugs throughout the city. Their chief rivals, I should say their only rivals, are another gang named the *Rabid Wolverines*. If your poet friend was accurate, Medford Smith may be getting his stash from the Siemens thugs."

"Any chance you can pinpoint for me where in particular this Siemens Gang hangs out along West Siemens Avenue?" Roger said.

"Hang tight," Wireless said. "I'm on it and will get back to you ASAP."

Before he disconnected from the call, Wireless made one last statement.

"Hey, not sure how Brett is doing with Chuck Richardson, but I'm getting a sense that the Tallahassee PD is heating up in their interest in the guy. An arrest may be pending, especially if they come up with any additional incriminating evidence they can use against him."

࿇

He woke up earlier than normal, despite the condition his head and body were in. The empty bottle of Black Jack Daniels was laying on the bed close to the .38 Chief's Special. He was glad that his wife was still out-of-town assisting her sister who had just had surgery.

Wayne McPherson was in his eighth year as an English teacher at Fulbright High School. Until now, until Michelle Landry, McPherson had never had any involvement with a student. The girl asked to speak with him after classes one day, at a time when she was struggling with a failing grade in his course. McPherson never suspected she would use an encounter with him to blackmail him into providing her with a better grade. He should have seen through what the girl was doing. He suspected that the girl might be using drugs. He did know what she was up to, but the urges she sparked in him were too much for him to resist.

He was only intimate with her the one time, but that was more than enough to hook him forever. Now, the girl was dead, and he had as strong a motive to kill her as anyone.

An empty bottle and a loaded gun on a night when his wife was not around was not enough for him to close the deal. His body shook. His head ached. He wondered just what it would take to bolster his confidence to do what he needed to do.

CHAPTER FOURTEEN

Strike Three

Miriam Walton was a sixteen-year-old student at Fulbright whose picture had proverbially been on a milk carton for months. That was when the girl disappeared. Following an investigation, the police took the position that the young cheerleader and her boyfriend, Lennie Foxx, who disappeared at the same time, had run away together. Miriam's parents, suspecting that Lennie was a druggie, had a major blowout with Miriam and forbade her from ever seeing Foxx again. Miriam and Lennie both disappeared the next day.

In the course of their investigation, the police believed, but could not prove, that Lennie was selling drugs working under Medford Smith and, thus, linked to the West Siemens Gang. Following a great deal of pressure from Miriam's parents and their attorney and based upon the fact that every effort to locate Lennie and Miriam had come up empty, the police agreed to re-open Miriam's case. Emily Walton, Miriam's mother, was of the opinion that Lennie Foxx kidnapped her daughter. Robert Walton, Miriam's father, questioned whether Miriam was the recent killer's first victim, even before Kelly Ann Lauren, but he did not openly express his fears in front of his wife. In either case, the Waltons were of the opinion that the police needed to do more than simply take the position that Miriam ran away with her boyfriend.

Brett booked a room at the same motel as Roger. He made a quick trip home, packed a few things, and would return to Tallahassee.

"Things are definitely about to get hot with Chuck Richardson," Brett told Roger. "This would be a good time for me to stay around."

Roger read the morning paper which carried the story about the reopening of Miriam Walton's case. While he was waiting for more insight on the West Siemens Gang from Wireless, Roger decided to see what, if anything, he could learn about Miriam Walton. He took a chance by visiting the Walton's home unannounced claiming to be a private investigator hired to look deeper into the recent murders. Emily Walton, Miriam's mother, was home alone when Roger arrived. The woman did not contact her husband or lawyer when Roger showed up. She was so pleased to talk with someone, anyone, interested in investigating the fate of her daughter. Emily invited Roger in and sat down with him in the living room.

"For months, I've been saying that I don't believe Miriam would run away. If anything, that Lennie Foxx would have forced her to leave with him and is holding my daughter against her will even now," Emily Walton said. "Finally, somebody is listening."

"Our goal," Roger said, "is to get to the truth. Your daughter's disappearance is every bit as important as the unfortunate events affecting the other students at Fulbright

High. You deserve the same degree of attention and investigative work from the police.

Tell me more about your daughter, Mrs. Walton. Help me get to know her so we can do a better job in searching for her. Don't limit yourself to her relationship with Lennie Foxx. Just paint a picture for me that I can use in anticipating what she might do in any given situation."

Emily Walton leaned forward, nodded her head, and gave rapt attention to Roger Clark. It was clear that she found his approach agreeable. She wanted to talk about her daughter and provide Roger with anything needed to solve the mystery of where Miriam was now.

"Miriam hated seeing others hurt or someone violating the standards of how things ought to be. That's why she reacted as she did when it came to Claire Waters."

"Claire Waters?" Roger said.

"Claire was on the girls' basketball team. Miriam learned that Claire was doing drugs, taking uppers or whatever they're called. Miriam reported Claire to Coach Trimble. As a result, Coach Trimble bounced Claire from the team. Afterwards, Claire left the school. Some people did not agree with what Miriam did, but she stood her ground. She said that the use of drugs could spread like a cancer and soon the whole team would be infested. Claire's brother, Hank, who was a year ahead of Miriam and Claire, also quit school and was particularly negative towards my daughter. But, you know, that's the kind of person Miriam is. She's not afraid to take a stand when she sees something negative going on."

Roger immediately questioned why a girl who would react strongly against a girl taking drugs would be dating a guy who her parents believed was a druggie, but he said nothing. He wasn't there to resolve any issues relating to Miriam Walton. He was in search of anything that might take the spotlight away from Chuck Richardson in the recent murders.

It didn't take Roger long to locate Hank and Claire Waters. The brother and sister were actually living together in an apartment on the other side of town from Fulbright High.

"You gotta be joking," Hank Waters said. He was sitting with Roger, along with Claire and her live-in boyfriend, Peter Grande.

"You got Miss Prissy, Miriam, reporting Claire here when all the girls on that team are getting uppers from Medford Smith. Truth is, Miriam resented my sister for stealing Miriam's boyfriend, Peter. And, let me tell you, when Claire was charged, she had enough class to never rat on her teammates. That's why she ended up being the only one thrown off the team."

"When you say everyone on the team was taking drugs, I assume you're also including Michelle Landry?" Roger said.

"Hell," Claire chimed in, "Michelle was probably one of the worst when it came to using stuff and influencing others. I admit that I took stuff, but I never considered it my mission to get the other girls involved. Michelle would sneak out at night and meet up with her supplier. They'd smoke weed and snort cocaine together."

"I assume by her supplier, you mean Medford Smith," Roger said.

"Medford's the one who supplied everyone at the school. Everyone trusted him," Hank said.

Hank and Claire were reluctant to identify the West Siemens Gang as Medford Smith's source for his drugs, but Roger's read on this was that they were aware where Smith's products came from.

"Michelle was getting greedy," Hank said. "The word we heard was that she started pushing for a cut on drugs Medford was selling to girls on the team. She said it was because of her that Smith had those girls as customers. She was threatening to talk about what was going on, even if she went down because of it."

"Now, ain't that something," Claire said. "First you got Saint Miriam snitching on me. Then, the next thing you hear she's dating a pothead, Lennie Foxx. Then, you've got Michelle Landry trying to go from user to dealer. And I'm the only one they end up throwing off the team. If that don't beat all."

∽

Roger informed Brett of all that he learned and made his next suggestion.

"I'd like to go talk to this Detective Wilson Jones. I had Betty Jo type up a summary of what I've learned, and have it delivered to me by courier. If Jones is as good as we think he is, he should take an interest in some of the things we're digging up. And he has the resources that we don't have to investigate deeper."

"Sure," Brett said. "Go for it, Rog. Just remember, our client is Tallahassee PD's primary or sole focus. We need to tread lightly with them."

∽

Roger felt a stroke of luck when he arrived at the police station and learned that Detective Wilson Jones was in the building. Roger's positive feelings ebbed considerably when after thirty-five minutes, he was still sitting in the foyer waiting for the detective to see him.

When Detective Wilson Jones did come out, he ushered Roger to his office. Roger introduced himself and explained why he was there.

"I've uncovered a few facts that I believe will be of interest to you in your investigation of these recent murders. I wanted to be sure to introduce myself and assure you that I, in no way, want to interfere in the work you are … "

Jones interrupted.

"That's exactly what you're doing, Clark. You're interfering in a police investigation. I already heard from Mrs. Walton. She believed when she spoke to you that you were working on behalf on this police department … "

"Whoa, hold on," Roger said, "I never represented … "

"No, you hold on, Clark. I could have you arrested right now and, at the same time, get your private investigator license pulled. You work for the attorney representing a major suspect in this case—a suspect we believe is the man responsible for killing these girls. Any attempt to sway or influence witnesses on behalf of your client constitutes obstruction of justice."

Clark's body was rigid. He clenched his jaw tightly.

"Listen, Detective. I've done nothing to influence anyone and haven't spoken to anybody about Chuck Richardson. And, I believe, if you do your homework, you'll damn well know that. Failure on your part to investigate some of the things I'm finding will be fodder for a smart defense attorney seeking to raise reasonable doubt in the minds of jurors."

Jones' nostrils were flared. His curled his hands into fists. He leaned forward, lifted a hand, and pointed an index finger at Roger's face.

"I don't need you to come in here and tell me how to do my job. I've been a detective long enough to know what the hell I'm doing."

"That's just it," Roger said, "you've got a strong rep of being a top-notch detective. I'd expect that means you don't close doors before thoroughly investigating and finding out what's behind every potential lead. I'm not an experienced detective like you, sir, but I didn't expect to find you unwilling to look into anything and everything related to your case."

Roger stood and faced Wilson Jones.

"I came here as a courtesy to hand over to you what I've learned. I have no intention whatsoever of interfering in the work you're doing or violating any laws. You want to arrest me, Jones, go ahead and do it. Meanwhile … " Roger tossed a manila folder onto the detective's desk. "here's a summary of what I've uncovered."

Then, Roger turned and walked out the door.

CHAPTER FIFTEEN

Gangs

"I'm speculating here, Brett, but I believe that Jones was in turmoil over whether Chuck Richardson is their man. He said he believed Chuck was guilty, but it sounded like a bunch of empty words. If it were up to him, Jones would be investigating this case a lot stronger than he currently is."

Roger Clark was speaking to Gatlin by phone reporting on his time with Detective Jones.

"Okay, well now we know what we're up against," Brett said. "It would have been nice to have Jones focused on more than our client, but that's not the cards we're being dealt. It'll be a lot more difficult if the police are locked into Chuck as the killer. Sounds like Jones is getting pressure from above—namely the chief detective and the district attorney. Be careful, Rog. Avoid anything that gives Jones cause to come after you."

"Yeah, will do, Brett. I'm not interested in seeing the insides of their local jail and I'll bet the food's not all that great."

Brett laughed.

"Hey, you'll bail me out if I get arrested, won't you, Brett?"

"Hmm, I guess I don't have a choice," Brett said. "It's not like I have time to find another investigator to work on this case."

The two men laughed together.

"While I was with Jones, Wireless left a message on my phone," Roger said. "I'll call the super-geek after I hang up with you. He was going to pinpoint who in the West Siemens Gang I need to talk with and where I can find these guys."

Brett hesitated before speaking. He had high regard for Rog's smarts and ability to handle himself. But, the idea of getting involved with a gang concerned Brett.

"I'm sure I don't need to tell you to watch your step. You don't want to mess with gang members. They become bold and aggressive when they know they've got others who'll back their play. Look, Rog, I know you can handle yourself, but these guys play dirty. Plus, if they're a major source for street drugs, they've got a lot at stake."

"I hear you, Brett, loud and clear. I don't intend to get into anything with these thugs. All I want is to get a sense of whether we've got something here that might be helpful when it comes to Chuck Richardson. If we have a whole basketball team involved with drugs and Michelle Landry was threatening to talk, we've got a bunch of people anxious to shut her up. Everything we're dealing with now may have started four months ago with the Walton girl and would have nothing to do with Chuck. And, somehow, it may include Kelly Ann Lauren."

"Okay, man," Brett said, "Judge Michaels wants the two attorneys in the Fessler case to come to his chambers this afternoon. I won't be in Tallahassee until sometime this evening."

"Alrighty then, Bubba," Roger said. "We'll leave the light on for you."

∞

Brett's time with Judge Michaels was shorter than he anticipated. He was well on his way to Tallahassee when a call came through on his cell phone.

"Mister Gatlin, this is Detective Wilson Jones. We are prepared to formally charge your client, Mister Charles Richardson, with two counts of first-degree murder. We're at the school where Mister Richardson works. We've confirmed he is here. I'm giving you notice, should you want to meet us at the station while we book the man."

"I'm on my way, Detective."

Brett called Jocelyn McCallister while he headed for the Tallahassee Police Department headquarters. She began to wail and sob at the news.

"Try to calm down, Jocelyn. We all knew this day was coming. We need to remain calm for Chuck's benefit. I'm on my way to the station. I'll check back with you afterwards. Remember, Chuck is going to need your support during this time until we clear his name."

"W-will th-they keep him locked up?"

Despite her frail emotions, Jocelyn needed to know the truth and prepare to accept it.

"I'm afraid so," Brett said. "With two charges of premeditated murder of young high school females, a judge is not going to grant bail."

Gatlin knew that Chuck, based upon his past claims of abuse at a mental health institution, would not fare well. He would need to be placed on suicide watch.

∽

The man followed Brett Gatlin onto I-10 East. He had no idea where Brett was going or whether he would be spending the night somewhere other than his home. None of that really mattered. He was focused upon Gatlin as his next victim and was being well-compensated for his work. He had just flown back into the area, so he had a small piece of luggage with him.

He almost blew it when he ventured outside Gatlin's home one night not long ago. Afterwards, he spotted the small well-hidden cameras that Gatlin had installed along with his house alarm. Thankfully, Gatlin had no reason to check the camera images and spot someone outside of his place. No problem. He'd eventually take care of things at some other location.

He'd already taken steps to make his presence known. In time, he would shake up Gatlin's world. That's when the fun would really begin. But for now, he would quietly go about his way planning, preparing, and strategizing.

∽

Detective Wilson Jones was seated alone in his office. He was agitated—struggling over who he should be angry with. He read through the material given to him by Roger Clark. In fact, he read through it three times. Roger Clark was right. A slew of questions arose in Wilson's mind. A significant portion of the basis for Chuck Richardson's arrest was influenced by the man's past. He reflected back on the conversation regarding Medford Smith.

If it's true that a team of young girls is involved with drugs, there's any number of people who would do anything to keep a lid on that. We could be talking about drug dealers, school officials, the coaching staff, the players, even some parents. Clark is right. This is the kind of thing that needs to be investigated. But Bradley made it clear that he believes we have our man in Richardson. We've got an antsy public, a critical media, and a number of elected officials, including the district attorney, who all want to see this thing end. My orders are to focus on Richardson, find more supportive evidence to nail this guy good, and not stir up any confusion by continuing a strong investigation of others. As the Chief Detective in the Homicide Division, Dan Bradley is my boss. Once he and the district attorney make a decision, that's it. Besides, rumor is that Bradley' going to move on and I'm in the best position to take over his job. If I cross the guy, I'd be putting my own career in jeopardy. Why would I do that? I've worked hard to get where I am today. Hell, I'm just gonna have to believe that Bradley and the DA have made the right call. Charles Richardson is our killer.

∽

West Siemens Avenue was certainly not a thriving neighborhood. Many of the stores in that area were out-of-business. Apartment buildings were in such disrepair they should be condemned and closed to occupancy. A number of abandoned vehicles were parked on the street—already stripped down for parts. Trash littered the neighborhood. Prostitutes walked the streets at night. And, of course, there were plenty of places where drugs were being sold.

Roger drove his Jeep to the corner of Siemens and Cypress. Wireless said the West Siemens Street Gang had their headquarters in an old building that once housed a Foley's Department Store. The leader of this gang was George "The Man" Mathis.

Before Roger exited his Jeep, one man stood at the driver's window, the other was at the passenger window. They both had a gun drawn and pointed at him. Roger stared back at the men, smiled broadly, and waved. Then, he opened the window and spoke to the man closest to him.

"Hey, there," Roger said, "can I help you with something? Used to be when you guys wanted money, you just cleaned someone's windshield with a dirty rag. Hold on, let me get a few bucks for you out of my wallet."

The man did not smile. He reached in through the window and grabbed Roger's throat. A tattoo on his wrist spelled out his gang name, which was Lancelot.

"I'd advise you to leave your hands right where I can see them."

"Sounds like excellent advice to me," Roger said.

Lancelot called over to the man at the passenger side window.

"We got us a funny man here, Cobra. Maybe we can get him to tell a few jokes before I put a bullet between his eyes."

The man ordered Roger to get out from his vehicle. Cobra came around, stood with Lancelot, and patted Roger down. He took Roger's gun and wallet.

"What makes you think you can come 'round here packin'?" Lancelot said.

"I came here," Roger said, "to meet with The Man."

Cobra shook his head and sneered.

"Nobody just shows up wantin' to meet with The Man. It don't work like that."

In turn, Roger looked each of these men directly in the eye. His posture was strong, with his shoulders back, chest out, and chin high.

"Look, get real, man. I don't have any other way of making contact with your boss. It ought to be clear to you that if I had something negative in mind, I wouldn't be here out in the open before the sun sets. I'm a private investigator working on the murders of the young high school girls. I've come across something your leader needs to know. He's got something I want. Means we're talking about a *quid pro quo*. I give and I get. It's as simple as that."

Cobra didn't understand the foreign language stuff this dude had spouted, but he did grasp that Roger felt he had something that The Man would want to know.

"Watcha got so important that The Man would be willing to see you, eh?"

"That's between me and him, but I guarantee he'd rather hear it from me than the police."

Cobra and Lancelot stood there in silence as they considered what their next move should be. Roger Clark did not frighten them. The Man did. The two men locked eyes. Cobra shrugged. Lancelot nodded and pivoted his head towards the front door of the West Siemens Gang building. Cobra grabbed Roger's arm and held it firmly, as Lancelot made a quick call. They started bringing Roger to the building, then stopped abruptly.

"Give me your cell phone," Cobra said. He took the phone and turned it off. "You ain't gonna be needing it when you talkin' with The Man—that's if he agrees to see you rather than have you and that Jeep of yours both dumped into the river."

Cobra and Lancelot laughed at Cobra's statement. Roger did not.

CHAPTER SIXTEEN

Been Around

Before Brett even arrived in Tallahassee, he called Roger. The phone was turned off. That made Brett uncomfortable, but he couldn't do much about it at the moment. He needed to be with his client while Chuck would be interrogated.

The police booked, printed, and formally charged Chuck Richardson. Then, they placed him alone in a cell. Chuck's eyes were feverish. He began to anxiously mutter to himself, while grabbing fistfuls of his hair and pulling. Detective Jones placed Chuck on suicide watch. Jones also called Gatlin and agreed to postpone any sessions with Chuck.

Brett, still unable to reach Roger, called Wireless and found out where Roger was headed on West Siemens Avenue. He parked a few blocks away from the corner of Siemens and Cypress. A small bodega was open. Brett went inside.

The shopkeeper was an elderly Latino man, about five feet six inches tall. Gray hair rimmed his bald head. Thick glasses were perched at the tip of his nose. The man was tearing open cigarette cartons and placing the individual packs on a shelf behind the counter. Brett picked up two packs of gum and walked to the cash register.

The man turned around facing Brett, took his money, and gave him his change.

"I'm looking for a friend of mine," Brett said. "Maybe you've seen him."

Brett began describing Roger, but the old man was shaking his head before Brett finished.

"No, we don't have nobody like that come around here," the shopkeeper said.

"I'm told that the headquarters for the West Siemens Gang is nearby," Brett said. "Is that true? You ever encounter any of those guys?"

The shopkeeper turned his back to Gatlin and continued with the job of placing cigarette packs on the shelves.

"*Mira señor,* in this neighborhood, nobody sees nothing. *Lo entiendes*—do you understand? You want to stay healthy, you don't see, you don't hear, you don't talk. You mind your own business. Even the police—they drive through sometimes, but they stay in their cars.

I tell you, it wasn't like that when I was young, but it's been that way for a long time now— ever since the people you talked about moved in.

If you know what's good for you, *amigo,* you will heed my advice, yes? Don't go around asking questions. It makes people nervous and that's not a healthy thing to do around here."

Brett nodded and stepped outside into the cool night air. A man walked past Brett. He stood around six feet four and weighed close to 350 pounds. He had a shaved head, scraggly beard, and menacing dark eyes. His sleeveless sweatshirt and the tattoos on his biceps identified him as a member of the

Rabid Wolverines Gang. His sweatshirt revealed that his nickname was *Mighty Joe Young.*

What happened next occurred so quickly that it took a moment or two for everything to register with Brett. Two men, even taller than the man who had just walked past Gatlin, came out from an alley. One of them plunged a knife into Mighty Joe's stomach and made a move to follow that up when they spotted a police car driving out on the street. The two men withdrew back into the alley as the police passed by, unaware of what had just occurred. Mighty Joe took a few steps then collapsed in the doorway of a shoe store. He sat on the cement with his back against the store's window. Brett ran over to the fallen man.

"Hey, hold tight, Bud. I'll call 9-1-1 and get you some help."

"No. No time for that," Joe responded. His breathing was labored. His hand covered the knife wound as blood continued to pour freely.

"You need to get out of here, man, if you know what's good for you," Joe said. "They're coming back to finish the job. Get out of here while you still can."

Too late! The two men were back. These two guys were like trees. Each was at least six feet six and every bit as brawny as Joe.

"You're standing in our way, dude," one of the giants said to Brett. "Move outta here."

Brett stood silently and stared back at the two behemoths. Joe started to make an effort to rise. Brett reached back, while keeping his eyes on the two Goliaths, and pressed down on Joe's head indicating he should remain on the ground. Joe stayed on the ground—not because he took Brett's advice. The man was unable to rise.

"We ain't telling you again, mister. That man is ours. If we need to take you out also, we ain't got a problem with that. This here's our last warning. Get outta our way."

Both men flicked open their switchblades and moved forward. Brett put a hand up with his palm facing the two men. As he spoke, his voice was calm and eerily confident.

"Okay, you've had your moment, now it's time for you to move on. There's no need for anyone else to get injured here, gentlemen. Let me make this really easy for you. All you need to do is turn around and walk away. Do that and you won't get hurt. We can end this thing peacefully right here."

One of the two men roared with laughter.

"You hear that, Butch? He's gonna let us go and not hurt us if we be good boys and walk away. That's really nice of him, don't ya think?"

Butch wasn't listening to his partner. He bared his teeth. His eyes were cold and flinty. His breathing was noisy. Butch, red-faced, and grunting, rushed towards Brett. Butch's partner, Rufus, followed suit. Butch thrust his knife at Brett, who moved to the side, and grabbed Butch's wrist. The snap that followed evidenced a bone breaking. Butch's knife fell to the ground. Brett whirled and high-kicked Butch on the side of his face, staggering the giant. He followed that with rapid punches to Butch's face and neck. A solid right cross started Butch's collapse to the ground, but, before he reached the cement, two solid overhand rights smashed against Butch's temple. The big man was not conscious when he landed face-down on the cement sidewalk.

Rufus was able to wrap his long arms around Brett from behind. He had Brett's arms pinned. Rufus held his knife in his right hand. With his arms pinned, Brett was still able to grab Rufus' right wrist. He held tight and prevented Rufus from lifting the knife. Perspiration formed on Brett's brow as he strained to keep the giant from lifting his arm. Then, Gatlin twisted the man's wrist, so the knife blade was facing Rufus' right thigh. Brett pushed hard as the knife plunged deeply into Rufus' leg. As Rufus reacted, Brett freed himself from Rufus' grasp, spun, and kicked the brute solidly in the groin. He followed that with several blows to Rufus' face and neck. The giant made one last effort to stab Brett by swiping the knife and cutting Gatlin's left arm. Brett continued to strike Rufus until the big man joined his partner on the ground.

Gatlin quickly turned back to Mighty Joe. He reached down to help the man to his feet.

"Let's go before anyone else arrives. I parked my car nearby. We've got to get you to a hospital. You're losing a lot of blood."

"No hospital," Joe said. "I've got another place."

Joe grabbed his cell phone and punched in a number.

"I need Zhivago waiting for me at his office now," Joe said. After a slight pause, he spoke again. "I don't care where he is or what he's doin'. I said now. Get him over there afore I bleed to death, you hear? I'm on my way."

Gatlin tucked his body under the bleeding man's shoulder. Brett grunted.

"Damn, why do you have to be so heavy?"

Mighty Joe started to bend over and would have fallen if Brett did not have hold of him. The big man's body shook. His breathing was hard and irregular.

116

"Who were those two guys who attacked you?" Brett said.

He had Mighty Joe distracted from his pain as they reached Brett's car.

"They're from the West Siemens Gang. We been havin' some issues with them lately. Hey, man, where'd you learn to fight like that?"

"Well," Brett said, "let's just say I've been around."

Brett was reminded that gang involvement resulted in the murder of his kid brother, but as he helped place gargantuan thug in the car, Brett knew this was not the time nor place to reflect upon his hatred for gangs. If he did, he'd leave this man on the streets to bleed to death and never would have defended him to begin with. Rather, this was a time for Brett to come to the assistance of another person—something he wished had been available to Derek before the police found his lifeless body in an alley outside of Nashville.

The ride to their destination took about twelve minutes. Brett used a towel he had in the car pressed against his passenger's bleeding wound. He was thankful that Joe was able to remain conscious and direct him. The doctor's office was in another seedy neighborhood in an older building nestled between a tattoo parlor and a smoke shop.

When they entered the front door, two men stood inside.

"Who's this dude?" one of the men said. "Only Wolverines supposed to know about doc."

"This guy is the reason I'm here instead of at the undertaker's," Mighty Joe growled. "He's okay. Just get me to doc while I'm still breathing."

The doctor stitched Joe up and gave him some shots and antibiotics that he would take with him. Then, the doctor examined Brett's arm. He cleaned the wound.

"You're not going to need any stitches. I'm going to give you some antibiotics now and send some with you. I want you to take them all as prescribed."

While the doctor worked on Brett, one of the gang members took Brett's wallet and checked his identity. Joe reached out and fist-bumped Brett.

"I owe you, dude."

"There's no debt here," Gatlin said. "You needed help and I just happened to be in the neighborhood. I'm here looking for my friend. Name's Roger Clark. He's a licensed investigator. Drives a Jeep and can handle himself. He was trying to meet with the West Siemens Gang."

"That ain't a smart move," Mighty Joe said. "Not a good idea at all. They ain't any tougher than us, but they're a whole lot ornerier. Like you seen tonight. I wandered too close to their turf and, if it weren't for you, I'd be on a slab in the morgue right about now."

"Yeah," Gatlin said. "Looks to me like I need to find Roger and get him out of here."

As Brett started to leave, one of the gang members grabbed his arm.

"Ain't nobody supposed to know about this doctor," he said.

"What doctor?" Brett said. "I don't know about any doctor."

Then, Brett walked out the door, got in his vehicle, and drove away.

CHAPTER SEVENTEEN

Quid Pro Quo

Cobra brought Roger through a large room where about twenty-five gang members were hanging out engaged in different activities. Some were seated at tables playing cards. Others were at a far corner of the room where several pool tables were located. A few others were watching television.

Roger noticed the closed door with a lone person standing in front of it and correctly assumed that was where George "The Man" Mathis was located.

"This here's the dude wants to see The Man," Cobra said.

The guy guarding the door knocked and opened it leading Roger to George Mathis.

It was apparent that Mathis had already been informed about Roger and told his guys to bring Roger to him. Roger caught the scent of weed. He spotted three people sitting in upholstered chairs passing a joint to each other. The youngest of the three, a man who appeared to be in his late twenties looked up at Roger. He was six feet tall, had chestnut brown hair, a handsome face, blue eyes, and neatly groomed facial hair.

"I hear tell you're looking for me," he said.

"If you're George Mathis," Roger said, "Then, you've got it right."

Roger moved a hand towards one of his pockets.

"I've already been searched twice by your men," he said, "so I assume nobody's gonna get spooked when I reach in for my credentials."

Roger pulled out his private investigator license and handed it to Mathis.

"So, you're a PI," Mathis said with a smile. "You know, I actually prefer PIs to cops—at least most of the time."

A wry smile covered Mathis' face as he handed Roger's credentials back to him.

"So, tell me, Private Investigator Clark, what brings you to me?"

"Well, like I told your two guys outside, I've been working on the case involving the recent murders of the high school girls," Roger said.

"Ah, terrible tragedy," George Mathis said. "Whoever is responsible for this needs to be publicly hanged. You know, I personally am in favor of public executions. In fact, I'd be glad to coordinate a public hanging once they catch the person."

Mathis chuckled and the two men seated nearby laughed along with him.

"Anyway, let's get back to my initial question. What brings you here to me?"

Roger remained standing in front of Mathis and the two other men. His eyes were dark and serious.

"In my investigation, I uncovered an association between a known drug dealer by the name of Medford Smith and the

Fulbright girls' basketball team. It's been suggested that you are familiar with Smith."

Mathis' body tensed. A vein in his neck became engorged as a redness took root in his face. The Man glared at Roger and spoke slowly and deliberately through gritted teeth.

"I would advise you, Clark, to be very careful with your words. Coming in here and telling me who I know or don't and implying that I have some kind of a relationship with a drug dealer upsets me. That's the kind of talk that can end up getting you in big trouble."

Mathis was leaning forward with his index finger pointed at Roger. An increased tension permeated the room.

Roger remained calm. He chose his next words carefully.

"I assure you that I meant absolutely no offense. I came here today to provide you with advanced notice about a situation that I believe you'd want to know about."

Roger was moving gingerly. He was bluffing. What he was about to deliver to Mathis was grounded in untruths. Roger assumed that Detective Jones had no recent contact with Mathis. Jones had already stated that he didn't intend to look beyond Chuck Richardson as the murderer of the high school girls.

"The police department criminal investigators," Roger said, "are privy to the fact that Medford Smith was providing drugs to the girls, including at least one of the victims in the murder case. They are of the opinion that you and your people are the source from which Smith gets his stash. This is not my opinion. I'm telling you what the police are thinking."

George Mathis glared back at Roger. He tightly shut his lips. He clasped his hands into fists and took a deep breath.

"So, why have you come here to me?"

"I want Medford Smith," Roger said. "I want to get to him before the Tallahassee Police do. If they can't find him, the police will come full force after you and your people. Truth is, they're not interested, at this time, in you. But, they're under incredible pressure to get some closure on these murders. The police are focused on one man. They've arrested our client. We believe the man is innocent. I believe Smith became aware that he was about to be outed and knew he had to silence the girls that are now dead. I'm asking you to deliver Smith to me."

Mathis leaned back in his chair. His face was tight. He clenched his jaw.

"And why would I do that, Mr. Clark?"

Roger had direct eye contact with Mathis.

"Keeps the cops away from you," Roger said. "They're not concerned right now with where Medford gets his stash. They're investigating murders."

The Man smiled.

"You fail to recognize that there is another option available to me, Investigator Clark."

Mathis made eye contact with his two gang members before turning his attention back to Roger Clark.

"If people like you and Medford Smith are no longer among the living, this issue ends up at a dead end."

Mathis laughed aloud. His men laughed with him.

✑

Brett stayed in his car driving cautiously through the neighborhood in search of Roger's Jeep. It was nowhere in sight.

Meanwhile, Roger had his arms cuffed behind his back and his mouth gagged, while seated in the passenger seat of his Jeep. West Siemens gang member, Cheesehead, a guy formerly from Wisconsin, was driving. A 2011 Ford F-150 truck with four additional gang members was following as Cheesehead headed towards the river.

Roger was already feeling the effects of the shot he'd been given once he'd been placed in the vehicle. His mind was swirling in the drug-induced stupor that had taken control of his senses. Cheesehead was speaking to him, not caring one bit whether Roger was coherent enough to understand what was being said.

"Haha," Cheesehead said, "The Man is really something, eh? He gets what he needs from you, then, presto, like a magician makes you and your vehicle disappear. You know, George Mathis took over the gang after his older brother, Justin, died in a car wreck. Mathis is young, but really wise and he ain't afraid to do whatever has to be done."

Roger knew he was taking a chance in coming into this gang's turf, but he was convinced that the police would not bother to look for Medford Smith. And if Smith learned that anyone was looking for him, he'd leave the area and be impossible to find.

Brett remembered that Roger had a GPS tracking device in his Jeep, but he did not know how to access it and search. He continued to call Roger, but never got an answer. As he searched the neighborhood, he grew increasingly concerned that Roger was in trouble. He made a phone call to Wireless.

"Roger has a GPS tracking device in his Jeep. Is that something you can identify and use to track where the Jeep is now."

"Hmm," Wireless said, "I'm gonna need some time to identify the unit."

"I'm afraid that time is the one thing we don't have," Brett said.

⧫

Cheesehead pulled the Jeep off the main road and drove down a dirt road that led to the shore of the lake. The Ford truck followed. Even before they reached the water, they caught the sulphuric smell with undertones of rotten eggs. When the Jeep stopped, Cheesehead stepped out of the driver's seat and all four men from the truck joined him. They pulled Roger out of his seat and threw him on the ground.

"Okay," Cheesehead said, "we got to make sure we get this dude unconscious. Then, we put him in the driver's seat and send him and his vehicle in for a nice underwater swim, eh? You guys bring the stuff to put him out?"

"Are you kidding?" one of the others said. "We already got him floating in happy land. Next injection and he goes into a freakin' coma. It's gonna look like he was so doped up, he lost control and ended up drowning hisself. Piece of cake. End of story."

"Okay, then, let's get it right, eh? We do it just like The Man ordered. I don't need to remind you guys that The Man, he don't like mistakes or sloppy work. You know what happens when somebody messes up, eh?"

One of the gang members named Lucifer walked over to Roger with a syringe in hand prepared to inject him. He leaned down and was ready to complete the task when he and the others were shocked to hear footsteps racing towards them. A half-dozen men bearing clubs, chains, and baseball bats showed up. Some were brandishing brass knuckles. Others had switchblades. They attacked the West Siemens Gang members with a fury leaving all five of them dead.

"Grab the dude and let's get outta here," one of the attackers said. "We can't take a chance the police gonna show up. We ain't got time and there's no way we gonna get that Jeep outta here. Ain't nobody knows it was us that done the fightin'. Even this dude here," he said referring to Roger, "don't know what happened. He's in some kind of la-la land."

The men drove away with Roger and headed back to their home turf. Mighty Joe Young, who was cousin to the gang leader, Moses, would be there at the headquarters still recuperating from his injuries. He had the men searching the area for Roger. When they spotted the Jeep and truck heading for the river, they knew they had found their man and found him just in time.

CHAPTER EIGHTEEN

Together Again

"So," Detective Jones began, "one of our patrol cars discovers five dead members of the West Siemens Gang on the shore of the lake and, lo and behold, a vehicle belonging to Roger Clark is also at the scene. What a surprise! Do either of you want to help explain what that is all about?"

Brett and Roger were with Detective Jones in his office taking turns staring at each other.

"Do you want to go first," Brett said, "or should I?"

"Well, it is my Jeep, so maybe I should be the one to start explaining things to the detective," Roger said.

"But, from what you told me," Brett said, "you weren't even fully conscious most of the time. I can't imagine you'd have much to say. I should go first."

"True," Roger said, "I was out of it. But, then, you weren't even there, so that's gonna limit your ability to explain things. Guess I go first."

"I don't know, Rog. You or me? Maybe, we should flip for it."

"You have any change in your pocket," Roger said. "Man, I never have any coins on me. Maybe I should start carrying a silver dollar in my pocket for times like this."

"Where are you going to get a silver dollar, Rog? I mean it's not like you'll get one as change from a grocery store cashier."

"Hmm, you gotta point there, Brett. Well, hey, forget the coin. Maybe we both start talking at the same time," Roger said.

Wilson Jones' nostrils were flared.

"You gentlemen may think this is a joke, but I assure you it's not. We've got five stiffs at the morgue that are members of a gang. In addition to me inheriting a multiple homicide case, our Department is now on full alert that we could have a gang war coming our way. So, whatever in hell you two know, it's time for you to stop playing around and get serious."

Roger's body tightened. He glared at the detective and spoke next.

"You didn't give a damn about anything or anyone else that might offset your obsession with charging Chuck Richardson with multiple murders. So, you put the burden on us, in order for Brett to fully represent his client, to investigate whether there might be someone else with a motive to murder those girls. I told you that I uncovered the fact that a guy named Medford Smith had been selling drugs to girls on the team, including one of the victims. And four months ago, Miriam Walton disappeared after she had exposed one of the girls as using drugs and threatened to reveal that Medford Smith was the supplier."

"And," Brett said, "what did you do with the information supplied to you by my investigator? Wait, hold on, don't strain yourself, Detective, I'll answer that for you. You did nothing.

You did absolutely nothing, despite the fact that the info given to you warranted a follow up. And the reason you did nothing is that you are focused only on Chuck Richardson as your killer."

"Exactly," Roger said, "so, based upon our belief that the source for the drugs sold by Smith was none other than the West Siemens Gang, I had to take a risk and go to them. I was trying to solicit their help in finding Medford Smith before he'd leave town."

"Pure and simple, Detective," Brett said, "if the truth is ever pure or simple, we have no assurance that you and your Department are conducting a full-scale investigation and not simply settling in on our client as the murderer. You helped place my investigator in harm's way because of your unwillingness to do your job."

"Yeah," Roger said, "word we had was that you're an exceptional detective with the experience and integrity to assure that anyone, including our client, involved in this case would receive a fair and honest investigation into who's guilty. Well, looks to me like that train left the station some time ago."

Wilson Jones was shifting in his chair, twisting his wedding ring, while avoiding eye contact with Brett and Roger. The minute or two of silence following the comments from Brett and Roger seemed like hours. Jones started to speak and stopped. Then he made eye contact with the two men and began to speak. His voice was much quieter now.

"So, what happened, Mister Clark, when you went to talk with the West Siemens Gang? I assume you met with them?"

"Feel free to call me Roger, Detective. When you mention Mister Clark, I start looking around the room for my dad and I lost him years ago."

Wilson smiled, as did Brett."

"Yeah," Roger said. "I ended up with George Mathis, the one they call 'The Man'."

"I'm familiar with him," Jones said. "I also knew his brother before him."

Roger's eyes looked downward. He shrugged, then spoke again.

"Look, I knew I was taking a risk going to a gang leader, but I was afraid we'd lose Medford Smith if I didn't do something quickly. I told Mathis that the police were looking for Smith and I wanted him before they found him. I implied that if Mathis didn't want a bunch of police officers breathing down his neck, it would be mutually beneficial for him to help me. I knew that if Smith is one of their dealers, they'd always know where he is.

I don't remember much after that. The hospital toxicology tests show that I was drugged. I have no recollection of how I ended up near the lake or what happened to the dead gang members. It seems safe to say the plan was to send me and my Jeep snorkeling, but the cavalry arrived just in time."

"And who is that cavalry," Wilson Jones said.

"That we can't answer," Brett said. "I was searching for Roger and found him wandering alone, aimlessly. I brought him to the ER."

Brett's statement that he found Roger wandering alone was a lie. The Rabid Wolverines found Brett and brought him to Roger at their headquarters. Detective Jones didn't believe

Brett's story, but he chose not to make an issue of it at this time.

"Look, Detective," Brett said, "we not only don't want to do your job, we readily admit we can't do it as well as you. But you have us in a quandary. I have an obligation to do all that I can to represent and defend my client. And, Roger and I are thwarted by a police department that's not doing its job and living up to its responsibilities."

Wilson Jones began looking around the room as if to assure that no one else was present. He started rubbing the back of his neck and swallowing excessively.

"Listen," Jones began, "I don't control everything around here. I have a chief detective and a district attorney who appraise criminal cases and make judgments that I have to abide by. I may not always like it, but that's the way things work here."

Gatlin paused before responding. He made eye contact with the detective and nodded with a gesture that indicated he understood what Jones was saying.

"Hey," Brett said, "we understand. But, there's one thing that you do control—you control yourself. You control your own integrity and how you're going to conduct yourself in any situation that you face. You can't overrule the chief detective or the DA, but nothing and no one can stop you from keeping an open mind, remaining objective, and refusing to completely shut a door until you're convinced that it should be closed. We're not asking you to take the position that Richardson is innocent. All we're asking is that you remain open to any evidence that might dispute the man's guilt."

Wilson Jones was nodding his head. His facial expression was soft, even conciliatory.

"I'm putting my career at risk here if my superiors believe that I'm undermining their approach and strategy, "Jones said.

Gatlin and Clark said nothing. Their faces were expressionless. Once again, an awkward, uncomfortable silence blanketed the room.

Jones stood, turned his back to the two men, and stared out a window. He placed his hands in his pockets and shook his head. Then, he whirled and faced the two men sitting in his office. He stretched out his hands towards Brett and Roger. He tightened his jaw and glared at the two men.

"I'm the only one here who has everything to lose. You guys are not in the position that I am. You're not... "

Gatlin stood. The reddening in his face and tightness in his eyes sent a message before he said another word.

"Get a grip, Jones. Don't give us this martyr crap. Who the hell are you kidding? We've got a client accused of multiple homicides. The man will either spend the rest of his life in prison or be put to death by the State of Florida and you have the gall to claim that you're the only one with something to lose? That's a joke. A job compared to a man's life—a man who may be innocent and lacks even the normal ability to defend himself."

Brett turned towards Roger.

"Come on, Rog, we're wasting our time here."

The two men began walking towards the door.

"Wait," Detective Jones said. "Please... come sit down."

Roger looked towards Brett, who nodded. They returned and sat down again.

"Okay, okay," Jones said. "I will consider and explore anything that I deem worthy of a look. You have my word on that. I'll do some additional investigation myself, but anything you bring to me will get my attention."

"That's all we ever wanted from you," Gatlin said. "We're not interested in creating any negative pressure for you when it comes to dealing with your boss or District Attorney Farragut."

"Alright," Detective Jones said, "let's find this Medford Smith and see what he has to say for himself. Meanwhile, I understand that you have confidentiality with your client," Jones said as he focused upon Gatlin, "but when it comes to other potential suspects, I want you to keep me updated on what you learn. If I'm going to do this, give me everything I need to do it right."

CHAPTER NINETEEN

Once in Every Life

It happened again the moment Tara answered the call. Brett's skin was flushed. His knees felt weak and a slow smile began to build upon his face. Tara could not see any of these reactions and Brett could not hear the increased beating of her own heart. Despite its impossibility, Brett thought he could smell the scent of Tara's perfume and see her alluring red lips. He would have given anything and everything to be with Tara rather than merely speaking to her by phone.

Tara chatted about a major civil suit she was handling. Brett provided a limited update on the Richardson case. Tara mentioned a movie she had watched on television the previous night. Brett talked about a book he intended to read once things slowed down.

Brett's heart was beating faster. His throat was dry. His hands were clammy. He was determined not to continue to hold back from Tara.

"Do you believe in people having a soul mate, Tara? You know, a special person that, I guess you could say, they were meant to be together with?"

Brett began rubbing the back of his neck and biting at his lips. He closed his eyes and took a calming breath as he awaited Tara's response.

"I do, Brett," Tara said. "I've always believed that love is something that doesn't come cheaply."

Brett hesitated before speaking again. Even as he did, another portion of his brain marveled at how locked up his emotions were. He knew that he would have a difficulty expressing feelings for another woman following Kerry's death. To do so, could serve as a betrayal of Kerry especially at a time when she was unable to respond in any manner.

But he reminded himself that Kerry was gone and he had to start living again.

"I-I thought that Kerry was that special person in my life, but that was clearly not to be. Afterwards, I assumed that a person gets only one shot at finding that one true love in their life. I-I was wrong, Tara. I realize that when you lose someone, another person *can* come along and *can* fill that special place in your heart. She's not a replacement or a substitute. She stands on her own, separate and apart from anyone else. Otherwise, she is not that uniquely special person.

I... never thought I would get a second chance to feel that special something for someone. I believed that I had my opportunity and that everything I ever wanted in life had passed me by."

Brett was rocking in place and shifting in his seat in an effort to get comfortable. Tara spoke next.

"Brett, I was engaged to a man who was a good person and someone I trusted and got along with. I broke off the engagement because that special something, that unique chemistry, just wasn't there. Our relationship simply progressed to a point where the next step was to get engaged and marry. I realized that I was settling for something less than true love. He was not my soul mate. Afterwards, I wondered if I would ever find that special person."

"Do you believe you ever will, Tara?"

Brett could not see the red blush that move into Tara's face. He could not see the tears that were filling her eyes.

She spoke softly, gently.

"I believe that I have, Brett."

A shock, like a bolt of lightning exploded within Brett's heart and mind. He paused just long enough to regain control of his breathing. The next step was his and he intended to take it. It was time to stop speaking in circles. He knew the course of action set before him and he took it.

"Tara, I was prepared to tell you that I am falling in love with you, but that is not true, not accurate, not an honest appraisal of things."

Brett stopped speaking for a moment and Tara held her breath. For a moment, she wondered if she had misread the situation between Brett and her.

"Tara, what I'm saying is that I am not *falling* in love. I'm already there. No, we haven't had a great deal of time knowing each other and we've only been together one time, but I know my own heart. I think of you every minute of the day. I can hardly breathe whenever I hear your voice. The more I learn about you, the more time we even just talk together, the more I love everything about you.

I love you, Tara. I know that I do."

✐

Hank and Claire Waters were at their apartment, along with Claire's boyfriend, Peter Grande, smoking a joint and feeling no pain when Medford Smith showed up with his partner, Walter Uriel. Walter stood at six feet five, with a strong body build. He neither smiled nor spoke. When he stared at someone, his eyes seemed to be crossed. It was apparent that he was one of Medford's body guards and enforcers.

"If it ain't our old friend, Medford," Hank said. "What got you out of your rat hole today?"

"This ain't no social visit, Waters. I hear that you and your sister been shooting your mouths off about me feeding drugs over to the girls on the basketball team. I got me a visit from the West Siemens boys. This upsets me, man. Upsets me very much. Makes me want to shut some mouths here."

Peter Grande stood and moved towards Medford. Walter Uriel grabbed Peter and threw him across the room causing him to fall to the floor.

"Oh yeah, forgot to mention," Medford said, "my friend Walter, here, he don't like nobody getting too close to me."

Claire was still sitting on the couch. Hank was standing. Peter was on the floor.

"Look, we don't want no trouble, Medford," Hank said.

"It's a little late for that, Hankie-boy. If you didn't want trouble, you needed to think about that before you started shooting your mouth off about me and drugs," Medford said.

Medford turned towards Walter, nodded, and gestured towards Claire. Walter reached down, pulled her from the couch, and wrapped his arms around her from behind.

"Maybe if Walter here has a little enjoyable time with Claire," Smith said, "you and your sister will get an initial taste of what happens to people who cross me."

Claire struggled in a futile attempt to get free from Walter.

"Let go of me. Get your filthy hands off me, you … "

Claire was unable to finish her sentence when Walter leaned his head over and covered her mouth with his lips. Hank made a move towards Walter and his sister when Medford pulled a switchblade from his pocket and pointed it at Hank. He shook his head and smiled.

"Uh, uh—bad idea, Hank. Best thing you can do right about now is chill, back off and enjoy the show."

No one was paying attention to Peter as he rose, pulled a knife from his pocket, and lunged towards Walter plunging the knife into the big guy. Claire howled and screamed. Walter spun around towards Peter. One of Walter's hands was covering the wound on his neck. With the other hand, he reached towards Peter. His hand grabbed the blade causing him to recoil. Walter was already light-headed, wobbly, and losing strength from the loss of blood. Within a few minutes, the big guy fell to the floor.

Medford's mouth fell open. Hank lunged towards him and struck Medford in the face. The two men grappled, Hank grabbed the knife, and stabbed Medford. A final thrust of the knife ended with Medford dead on the living room floor.

Hank, Claire, and Peter all stood and stared at the bodies of Medford and Walter, stunned at what had occurred. Claire was sobbing. Peter held her in his arms.

"W-we need t-to find a w-way to clean th-things up here and get rid of these b-bodies," Hank said.

Then, he turned his head to the side, bent over, and vomited.

℘

His wife would be back sometime tomorrow. He was surprised that he had not yet heard from the police. Then again, how would they know about his involvement with the dead girl? He certainly had never told anyone. Had she? Had Michelle Landry left any evidence behind—a notation in her diary? Or had she told others what happened. Young girls like her enjoyed bragging about their conquests—especially when it involved a teacher.

Wayne McPherson knew that the smart tactic would be to do nothing. There was no indication that anyone was aware of his one-time fling with Michelle. Even if she had told someone or left some kind of note behind, he would deny that anything ever occurred between the two. He could take the position that whatever she claimed was nothing more than the fantasies of a foolish young girl or, a contrived plan to blackmail him one day if she was in danger of failing his course. But he would state that he did help her grasp what she needed and her grades had dramatically improved.

He had calmed himself down and convinced himself that all would be fine, when a combination of too much whiskey and the terror that raged within him set him off again. Why had he been so foolish and put everything at risk? His marriage, his career, his very reputation all hung on whether a drugged up, immature girl with a body that appeared to be ahead of its years somehow left evidence behind of what he had done. His body shook violently as he began to sob.

Once again, the .38 Chief's Special was nearby. Once again he pressed it against his temple as he had done several times before. Once again, he placed his finger on the gun's trigger.

Unlike before, he squeezed the trigger. Wayne McPherson's wife would find his dead body the following day when she returned home. He did not leave a note. No one had any idea why he took his life.

CHAPTER TWENTY

On the Job

In the morning, before Brett had even showered and left his motel room, he received a call from Detective Wilson Jones.

"Just want to inform you, Counselor, that we found Medford Smith, but he isn't going to be talking to us or anyone else."

"How's that?" Brett said.

"We found Smith's body and one of his thugs, a guy named Walter Uriel, on the shore of the pond in Bryant Park. It appears as if they both were stabbed to death. We also believe the bodies had been moved. Where they were found was not the crime scene."

Brett was silent as he considered what the death of Smith meant. It certainly curtailed any possibility of questioning him in the deaths of the high school girls.

"Any chance this was the work of the West Siemens Avenue Gang?" Brett asked.

"Too early to know anything," Jones said. "We're just starting our investigation now. Okay, gotta go, just keeping my end of the agreement here in filling you and your partner, Roger, in on the latest."

༲

The murders of Medford Smith and Walter Uriel prompted Detective Wilson Jones to visit the Landry home. He did not know if Doctor Holden Landry and his wife, Lisa, were aware of Michelle's involvement with Medford Smith, but it was time to find out.

Jones did not believe that the West Siemens Avenue Gang murdered Smith and Uriel. The murders were sloppy and didn't fit the pattern of a gang killing. Jones was aware that Doctor Landry had motive to kill Medford Smith. He had a lot to lose in terms of his reputation and standing in the community. Landry had announced his candidacy for a top administrative position in the county's largest hospital. The man certainly would not want Medford Smith spouting his mouth off about the Landry girl having been one of his major clients.

Doctor Landry glared at Detective Wilson. His jaw was clenched tight and his eyes were narrowed.

"I'd advise you to be very careful Detective with any insinuation that our daughter had anything to do with illegal drugs. And, I've already made it clear to you that my wife and I have never heard of someone named Medford Smith."

Lisa Landry was already in tears when she spoke next.

"Isn't it enough, Detective Wilson, that we have lost our daughter, without you now destroying her reputation?"

Jones held a hand up with his palm facing Doctor and Mrs. Landry.

"I assure you, I am not interested in casting any negative aspersions towards your daughter and will not treat her character lightly. I'm sharing some of these things that have come up in our investigative work in an effort to explore whatever we can to find out who is responsible for your daughter's death. I'm interested in finding a killer, not in questioning your daughter's reputation. I give you my assurance that I will treat matters related to Michelle with the utmost sensitivity."

Holden and Lisa Landry were appeased by Jones' apparent respect for their daughter's name. Jones, on the other hand, was not able to completely rule out either of them as a suspect in the murders of Smith and Uriel. He was leaning towards the fact that Michelle's parents either did not know or were in denial about her drug involvement. Holden Landry came across as a narcissist whose primary focus was upon himself and his own career. It was no surprise to Jones that the man might not be particularly aware of his daughter's activities.

※

Chief Detective Dan Bradley glared at Wilson Jones. His lips drew back in a snarl. He lifted his right hand and pointed his index finger at the detective's face.

"You... Let me tell you, Jones, both Bill Farragut," Bradley said, referring to the DA, "and I got a call from an irate Doctor Landry. What in the hell were you doing talking to one of the most prominent citizens in our city and accusing his deceased daughter of being a druggie? First of all, I thought we made it clear that we've got our man. He's sitting in our jail, damnit. I thought we all agreed on that? How in the hell did you miss that message?"

Bradley rose from his desk chair and was now standing over the seated Wilson Jones—much too close for Jones' liking. Bradley's face was red. His teeth were bared and his eyes protruding. Spittle flew from his mouth as he spoke.

"You think that you should be the chief detective, huh? Is that what this is about? You're already campaigning for my job? What? You want to be noticed? The media can refer to you as the detective who never quits working a case no matter what? Matter of fact, why don't you call in the press? You can give an exclusive interview—let everyone know that Wilson Jones is smarter than his boss, smarter than the DA, hell, smarter than everybody."

Bradley turned his back to Jones, reached over, and picked up the coffee cup that was on his desk. He flung it against the wall and watched as it shattered. The pieces fell silently onto the carpeted floor. Then, he whirled around facing Wilson Jones again. He extended his right arm towards Detective Jones and pointed his finger again directly at the man's face.

"I'm warning you, Wilson. You're on thin ice. I should charge you with insubordination and throw you the hell out of here. Now, you listen and listen good. You focus on Richardson. We're only interested in building the case against him. You hear me?

And, if you know what's best for you, you won't even think of doing anything that embarrasses me or Farragut."

Bradley broke the eye contact he had with Jones, lifted a napkin from his desk, crumpled it, and dropped it into the wastepaper basket.

"Now, get the hell out of here," Bradley said without even looking at the detective, "before I take your damn badge and put you out on the street among the unemployed."

Wilson Jones left Bradley's office. Everything within him was screaming in anger. He was livid at being treated like a child in the school principal's office. He believed he was at a point in his life and career where he should never be berated and demeaned as Bradley had done. In fact, no employer or supervisor ever has that right.

The man has no business talking to me like that. I won't let Bradley or Farragut hold this job over my head. I'm employable. I have the experience, an outstanding employment record, and the personality to get a job in another police department with no problem, whatsoever. I'm trying to maintain my poise, but, I swear, if Bradley ever pulls that crap on me again, he's liable to find my fist down his throat. Don't ever threaten me with my job.

No, Detective Jones wasn't fighting for his job. Rather, he was fighting to maintain his integrity and his dignity. Ever since he became a police officer, Wilson Jones had never crossed the line. He'd never falsified evidence, taken a bribe, played politics with an arrest, nor arrested someone just because he was told to do so.

Jones was not finished with this case. If he was going to take the stance that Chuck Richardson was guilty, Wilson Jones would do so because he believed the evidence supported that position—not because the chief detective or district attorney were bullying him. Nobody was going to take away his integrity and character—not now, not ever.

༄

Brett and Tara were talking again on the phone. He asked if there was any way she could take even a weekend and fly into the Pensacola area for a visit, but Tara's caseload and scheduled hearings and meetings didn't provide her with any opportunity to do so. But he and Tara agreed that they would find a way to see each other again soon.

"First chance I get when I'm not in Tallahassee," Brett said, "I'm going to take a ride over to Navarre Beach and FaceTime you. I'll show you the awesome white sand beaches in our area. When I keep the phone active and drive along Via de Luna over to Pensacola Beach, I'm sure I can lure you into this area."

Tara laughed.

"Brett, if you're there, that's all the incentive I'll need to come."

Brett's face was flushed. He felt like a schoolboy flirting with a pretty girl on the playground.

"You keep mentioning our beaches in the Panhandle," Brett said. "I had no idea that a girl from Indiana would be so crazy about sand and beaches."

Tara laughed.

"What'd you expect? That I would only go gaga over corn and wheat fields?" Tara said, generating laughter from Brett.

"I mean get real, Brett, beaches are big-time America, sir. Most everybody loves beaches. They're a real part of the lure that Florida has."

"Aha! So, you do admit that beaches can lure you into this area."

"Yes, indeed," Tara said. "Second only to your own personal magnetism."

Brett and Tara both laughed heartily. He marveled at how incredibly easy Tara was to talk with and enjoy.

"Okay," Brett said, "here's the deal. When you do get to come into this area, I'll make sure we have plenty of beach time."

Tara laughed again.

"Perfect, as long as it includes Brett time."

CHAPTER TWENTY-ONE

Still Searching

Crawfordville is some eighteen miles from Tallahassee and a drive of slightly less than thirty minutes. Detective Wilson Jones would readily admit that using an oyster bar in that community for a meeting place might seem to be overkill, but he had to be sure that he didn't tip his hand to Bradley or Farragut. Although he made a decision not to buckle under their threats that he not continue his investigative work, he was not going to risk being discovered and fired before he completed his work.

When Brett and Roger arrived, they spotted Detective Jones seated a table in a far corner of the room. The three men greeted each other with simple head nods and hand shakes. Jones had asked them to meet with him, but he never explained why he wanted the three of them to get together. He wasted no time in doing so now.

"I know that you both were frustrated that I seemed to be unwilling to continue my criminal investigative work in the recent murders of the high school girls," Jones said. "Of course, I understand that you have a bias and vested interest in defending your client."

"Look, before you proceed with that comment hanging in the air," Gatlin said, "we do represent Charles Richardson. But, as we've stated before, we're not asking you or anyone else to help us prove that this man is innocent. We just want to know that you and your people haven't curtailed a thorough investigation just because you believe you found the right person. It should be no surprise to you, Detective, that the police have been known to stop their investigative work once they've zeroed in on a particular suspect."

"That's right," Roger Clark said, "and sometimes, say in a homicide case, afterwards when their primary suspect is proven innocent, the police have nothing left but a cold trail in the search for the real killer."

"I hear you. I hear you," Wilson Jones said. "I asked you to meet with me here today because we're beyond the question of whether I'm willing to continue with my investigation. And, I say that even though your client has been arrested and is now in custody. I asked you to meet me today because I need your help."

"That's interesting," Brett said. "Of course, we'll assist in any way we can, but can't imagine what you need from us."

"Yeah," Roger said, "it's not every day that an experienced detective would solicit the assistance of a lawyer and investigator. You guys are known to be unwilling to even cooperate between one law enforcement agency and another. The way I see it, y'all tend to be more territorial than a pit bull."

Jones and Gatlin both chuckled at Roger's comment.

"I suppose that even a pit bull would wish he had some help if he's cornered and working completely alone," Wilson Jones said.

"What do you mean by that?" Roger asked.

Jones hesitated. He tilted his head from side-to side, then rubbed a hand through his hair. He sucked in a deep breath and then slowly released it. The man appeared to be seeking the right words before speaking again.

"I'm putting my career on the line here. I need to know whether you both are genuinely seeking to uncover the truth or opportunists who will hold back on nothing just to advance your interests."

Brett Gatlin stared into Jones' eyes. He sensed a vulnerability in the man. He was convinced that the detective was conflicted. If Brett was reading things correctly, Jones was caught between his personal integrity and the risk of putting his career and future at stake.

"Detective, I'm sure you're aware of my background and what I went through when I was falsely accused of crimes I never committed. My life, my reputation, my personal character were all torn apart. All I can tell you, sir, is that I'll never let anyone take away from me the very standards that I live by. Never. Personal integrity is something I will not compromise. And I know that Roger feels the same. If you're questioning whether we can be trusted, the answer is an unequivocal yes. You alone have to decide whether you're willing to believe that."

The silence that followed Brett's statements hung in the air and generated an awareness that a proverbial line had been drawn in the sand. If Detective Wilson Jones would not or could not accept what Brett was saying, there would be no need for continuing this meeting. It was no longer a question of whether Jones was willing to trust and work with Brett and

Roger, it was also a question of whether they would be willing to work with him.

Jones nodded his head. His facial expression softened and were accompanied with a curt nod and strong eye contact.

"I trust you both," Wilson said.

Detective Jones paused before sharing what was on his mind. He was a private man, a solitary person. The only person he ever made himself vulnerable to was his wife, Bianca. He came oh-so-close to not continuing with what he wanted to say, but, took a deep breath and spoke.

"As you know, Chief Detective Daniel Bradley heads up the detective division in the Tallahassee Police Department. He's my direct supervisor," Jones said. "As I told you before, Bradley and District Attorney William Farragut will make the final call on the disposition of major criminal cases. Bradley reviews the work of his staff, Farragut decides whether there is enough to go forward to seek a conviction. That's standard operating procedures."

"But something's different in this case, I assume," Brett said.

Jones focused his eyes downward before lifting them and staring away. He reached down and lifted the salt shaker from the table and began to twirl it in his hands.

"I don't know what it is. Bradley was livid when he learned that I had even considered talking to the parents of one of the homicide victims and pursuing the subject of whether their daughter might have had some involvement with drugs," Jones said. "You know, I can understand that a DA wants closure on a case and another feather in his cap, especially when it comes to a man like Farragut. It's no secret to anyone that he has additional political aspirations. But I've never seen Dan Bradley react like this. There's something more going on, but I have no idea what it is and I'm in a difficult position to do the kind of investigation I would want to do."

"Meaning it would help if we could dig in and see what we might find," Roger said.

Jones bowed his head for a moment, lifted it, looked away, then focused back on Brett and Roger.

"Yes," Jones answered, "that's precisely what I mean."

Gatlin formed his hands into a steeple, pressed his lips together, and made strong eye contact with Detective Jones.

"Okay, so here's the deal. We'll see what we can come up with regarding Chief Detective Bradley and Farragut and we'll be careful to in no way implicate you in what we're doing should anyone ever find out. We'll keep you apprised as to what we learn."

"And if anything comes up on my end that might be of value for you in defending your client, I will let you know, as long as I can do so ethically," Jones said.

Gatlin nodded, reached out, and shook the detective's hand.

"One more thing," Jones said as he made eye contact with Brett and Roger. "How about you drop the title and call me Wilson."

❧

The sound of sneakers squeaking as they rubbed against the gymnasium floor meshed with the female voices calling out plays and positions to one another. Once again, he positioned himself where no one, including Coach Trimble, would see him watching the girls as they practiced in the school gym. He loved seeing them in their shorts. He enjoyed seeing the perspiration bleed through their clothing as they hustled back and forth on the floor. He didn't really care if they sank any baskets or demonstrated any skillfulness. He just enjoyed watching them. He hoped that the girls would continue practicing and playing their games this year. He even knew which of the girls he would choose.

Coach Hal Trimble was in his eleventh year of heading up the team. He had three state titles, eight conference championships, and a winning season in every year except for his first to show for his efforts. He saw some value in letting the girls play to help take their minds off the horrible tragedies that had occurred.

The question of whether the Fulbright girls' basketball team would continue their season was still up in the air. A meeting was scheduled that would include the school board members, the principal, other school officials, Coach Trimble, and the girls' parents. They would discuss this issue and help the school make its determination. Meanwhile, Trimble was still conducting practices. He wanted, in some way, to help his girls get through this time in their lives.

CHAPTER TWENTY-TWO

Much Too Close

Despite the fact that Brett and Roger had separate motel rooms, each room had two double beds. That worked perfectly now as the two men were each seated on a bed in Roger's room with sandwiches, chips, and cans of beer. They had decided to use this time in a more secure environment to discuss their strategy.

The discussion with Wilson Jones in Crawfordville served to encourage and forewarn the two men. Jones' willingness to continue the investigation was a breath of fresh air and an impetus to their own efforts to clear Chuck Richardson of these heinous crimes. The stance that DA Bill Farragut and Chief Detective Bradley had taken regarding the arrest of Chuck Richardson appeared to be without compromise. The reaction of Chief Detective Bradley if he learned that they were now going to dig deeper into his life was a major concern.

"Wilson Jones is not a coward," Gatlin said, "but he's clearly nobody's fool. He knows anyone who puts themselves on the wrong side of Bradley and Farragut will be playing with fire. We've got to be super careful, Rog. There's no room for error here."

Roger finished chewing on a bite from his sandwich and took a quick slug of beer.

"Man, I hear you loud and clear, Brett. Sound like Bradley was all over Jones when he learned that the man was still investigating other suspects. No telling what Bradley would do if he learns that we're working with the detective and not only continuing the investigation—we're investigating Bradley. Who knows? I may have an old unpaid parking ticket those dudes will uncover and next thing you know, I'm wearing orange and sitting behind bars."

Brett chuckled along with Roger.

"Yeah, with nobody, including me, knowing where you are as the years pass by," Brett said followed by a laugh.

"And to make matters worse," Roger said, "orange is not my best color."

◦∕∕◦

Chuck Richardson was continually pacing the floor and muttering to himself in the small jail cell he was confined in. He remained under a suicide watch. For now, Chuck's only times out of his cell were when his sister Jocelyn visited him.

"I'm really worried about him," Jocelyn told Brett. Chuck's not eating, he's already lost a lot of weight, and I find that he's not as alert mentally. I honestly believe he's haunted by past memories of when he was placed in that mental institution."

"Yeah, exactly what we were afraid of. I've petitioned the judge again explaining the uniqueness of Chuck's position based upon his borderline intellectual functioning and past negative experiences. We haven't gotten a ruling yet, but, frankly, I'm not overly confident that we'll get a positive response. Even if the judge agrees with us, he doesn't want to appear to be granting any leniency to a man charged with these crimes. The public outcry against that would be devastating to a judge's career."

"I'm telling you, I'm scared. Chuck is so incredibly vulnerable. I just don't know how long he'll last where he is now."

Brett did not respond to Jocelyn's statement. He agreed with her and did not want to further alarm her.

Wireless was using his incredible computer forensic skills to dig deeper into the life of Dan Bradley, while Brett and Roger were waiting for some feedback.

"Bradley doesn't know what we're up to, he doesn't even know that Wireless exists and yet I'm edgy, concerned that all of a sudden he becomes aware of everything," Roger said.

"Well, I know it's harrowing when you consider that we're dealing with the chief detective of a large municipal police department," Brett said. "And, we don't know what we're looking for. But, we honestly have no choice, Rog. All we know is that there has to be something more to cause an expetrienced chief detective to be acting the way Bradley is. And our client's life is at stake as a result of Bradley closing his eyes to any suspect other than Chuck Richardson."

Roger nodded his head.

"Man, I totally agree with the fact that there's something going on with Bradley," Roger said. "What makes this even more confusing is that we had Wireless run a background check on Bradley at the same time we were checking out Wilson Jones. Bradley came up clean with such an exemplary record in law enforcement that I considered writing a letter to the Pope recommending the man for sainthood."

Brett laughed.

"So, why didn't you do it?"

"Well, for one thing," Roger said, "the man's not dead yet. As I understand things, and I'm certainly no expert on the subject, you gotta be expired before you can even be considered for a halo."

The laughter that ensued between the two men was interrupted by a call from Wireless that came through on Roger's phone.

Wireless had not yet celebrated his twenty-third birthday. He was everything that one might expect from certain computer geniuses who use their skills as the essence of their personality. He was a computer geek, a loner, a socially maladjusted young man who was incredibly comfortable behind a keyboard and a monitor, but at a complete loss in social situations. He called himself Wireless, never revealed his true identity or physical location to anyone, and hardly, if ever, spoke on a phone to people he worked with. Kerry Anderson, the Washington Post reporter who introduced Wireless to Brett and Roger, reached into the young man's life as no one had before, even though they never physically met one another.

"Kerry, she was a special lady," Wireless once told Brett. "She believed in me when nobody else did. To a lot of others, I'd be nothing more than a weird computer geek. But, Kerry, she treated me with such respect. I didn't work with her just for the money I got paid. I worked for her because she was one of those rare individuals who sometimes grace this dark, evil world we live in. And, I'll tell you something, man. Once I got to know her, it wasn't just a question of Kerry believing in me. I believed in her."

Roger mouthed Wireless' name to Brett as he answered the call.

"Hey, Data Man," Roger said, "Brett and I were just talking about you or … uh … were you maybe listening in on us without us knowing?"

"Very funny, Captain America," Wireless said. "The only listening I ever do has something to do with computers and bytes, and, of course, my unique ability to go where others cannot and dare not tread."

"So, whatcha got for us, Lord Terrabyte?" Roger said. "Anything exciting? I'm anxious to get to work. Besides, I've gotta justify my paycheck before attorney you-know-who gets antsy."

Wireless laughed. The computer whiz was not known to engage much in humor, but Roger had clearly been a major influence in getting Wireless to open up much more. Plus, the fact that Brett and Roger were so closely aligned with Kerry increased the trust that Wireless had in these two men.

"It took me a while and some pretty sophisticated digging, but I've come up with something that may be of interest to you guys. I can't say whether it has anything to do with this current homicide case at all, but I'll leave that to you and your expertise. Anyway, I've compiled a report with what I've found."

"Great," Roger said, "Send it on over to my phone and Brett's and we'll have a look."

"You got it," Wireless said. "Should be there in 1-2-3."

Roger heard the sounds emanating from his phone and Brett's informing them that Wireless' findings were available to them. Wireless disconnected after assuring the two men he would continue to search for anything having to do with Bradley and DA Farragut.

Since Wireless had already searched the career background of Chief Bradley, his current efforts were focused on the man's personal life. Brett and Roger each read through the material before discussing anything with each other. They learned that Bradley was born in Jacksonville, Florida. The family moved to Tallahassee when Bradley's father took a job at the Tallahassee International Airport. After graduating high school, Bradley took some courses at the Tallahassee Community College but did not earn a degree. He worked his way up through the ranks of the Tallahassee Police Department.

Dan Bradley's first marriage ended in divorce in less than three years. The couple had no children. His current marriage was in its twenty-second year. He and his wife, Patricia, have three children. Kyle, their middle child, was a senior at Fulbright High School.

Initially, Wireless' report was a basic overview of facts related to Bradley's personal life. The final segment contained material that was uncovered by Wireless in sites not available to the general public. This was where Brett and Roger learned about Kyle Bradley.

"Okay," Brett said as he looked up from his version of the report and spoke to Roger. The two men continued to glance at

Wireless' report as they openly discussed what they were seeing. "So, apparently Kyle Bradley got himself into some trouble when he was fifteen with a girl named Rebecca Norman. She was also a student at Fulbright."

"Yeah, I see that," Roger said, "and the records were expunged due to the fact that Kyle and the girl were both minors. In fact, Rebecca was a year behind Kyle and only fourteen at the time."

"And from what Wireless discovered, the girl withdrew from Fulbright," Brett said. "and the family moved away to Crestview—that's only about thirty minutes away from Milton. Hey, Rog, take a look at what Wireless says next. He's showing a report from Fulbright High that Kyle Bradley has not been in class in over three weeks."

"Yeah," Roger said, "I spotted that, but since the kid is now eighteen, he hasn't been reported as truant, even though, if he has withdrawn, he would be required to formally notify the school of that decision."

There were no missing person reports, no evidence that Kyle was ill, nothing to indicate that the school had, as yet, taken any formal action to report Kyle's absence, and nothing that Wireless found to indicate that Dan Bradley and his wife were concerned about this.

"This may not amount to anything, Rog, but I believe we need to dig in here and find out why a chief detective's son has disappeared, and no one seems to be reacting. Only problem is that I'm not sure where to start with this. We sure as hell can't talk with Bradley or his wife or even the school without generating a whole lot of flack."

Roger sat quietly with a pensive look on his face. He tossed his phone down on the bed he was sitting on.

"The only thing I can think of, Brett, is to go backwards before we even try to move forward. There are some facts that we do know that have nothing to do with talking to the Bradley and his wife or any school officials."

Brett nodded his head.

"I assume you're saying it's time to have a chat with some people over in Crestview," Gatlin said.

Yeah," Roger nodded. "I ran a search for directions to the Crestview address provided by Wireless. I believe it's time to have a talk with the Normans."

CHAPTER TWENTY-THREE

Looking at the Past

Brett went with Roger to Crestview to meet with the Normans. Brett was driving. Roger was following up texting back and forth with Wireless in an effort to glean some additional insight on the Norman family. Brett's phone rang. The caller was Detective Wilson Jones.

"Need to inform you that we have a search warrant to inspect the bedroom at the McAllister home where Charles Richardson has been staying and the man's vehicle at that residence. I'm sending a copy of that document to your phone now."

Brett pulled over for a moment to read the document.

Wilson Jones granted Brett a few extra minutes to inform Jocelyn McAllister. Jones and a team waited in their vehicles outside Jocelyn's home. This courtesy was geared towards avoiding any major issues when they appeared at the front door. The time they extended was short, so as not to provide Jocelyn with an opportunity to enter her brother's bedroom and remove any items that might be incriminating. At the same time, two officers went behind the house where they would initially wait for Jocelyn to bring them the keys to Chuck's car.

The search warrant was, as Detective Jones had stated, limited to the bedroom where Chuck was sleeping and to his car, which was still parked behind the house.

Brett was talking with Jocelyn on the phone.

"Okay, Jocelyn, the warrant is valid. They have authority from a judge to search Chuck's room and his vehicle—nothing else. If they even attempt to search elsewhere, call me immediately. Otherwise, don't interfere. Just let them do what they came for. If you have any questions, call me."

Brett then contacted Detective Jones.

"Thanks for the courtesy. You're good to go."

That same day, a police car was parked outside of Chuck Richardson's apartment. It's occupant would remain eyes-on throughout the night to assure that no one attempted to enter that unit. Based upon another warrant, Chuck's apartment was searched.

༄

Howard and Elaine Norman lived in a four-bedroom brick home in a pleasant subdivision in Crestview. They were an older couple who adopted Rebecca when they were both already in their late 40s. That was when they finally accepted what they had been told years earlier. They could not have children of their own. Upon hearing from Brett, they both agreed to sit with him and his investigator. Rebecca was at school.

Howard was tall at six feet three. He was thin, had a high hairline, without much hair anyway, and wore wire rimmed glasses. Elaine stood at five feet eleven. Her gray hair extended to just above her shoulders. She had a friendly pleasant face with dimples that accentuated her smile. Her blue eyes were warm and inviting.

Elaine offered coffee, iced tea, or soft drinks to the two men, which they politely refused. Brett and Roger sat with the Normans in the living room.

"We didn't want Becca to be here when we had a discussion with you," Howard said. "Even though it's been a few years since it all happened, she still bears the scars of it all. We try to help her to get past the hurt she endured."

"Well," Elaine said, " 'endured' may not be the best choice of words. Having a child with a father who's had no involvement during the pregnancy or since has been difficult for Becca."

Elaine immediately spotted the look on Brett's and Roger's faces.

"You don't know, do you?" she said.

"We're aware that there was an incident between your daughter and Kyle Bradley, the son of the Tallahassee Police Department Chief Detective," Brett said, "where you, as Rebecca's parents, lodged a complaint that the Bradley boy had nonconsensual sex with your daughter."

"Forget the damn nonconsensual crap," Howard said. "He raped Becca is what happened. He took advantage of her, forced himself on her, and raped her."

"She liked Kyle Bradley," Elaine said, "but had never dated him or anything. They were at a party. The kids, even though underage, were drinking. Becca was not used to drinking, but, as kids are prone to do, she didn't want to be looked upon negatively by her peers. So, she partook, also. She admits that it didn't take much for her to start feeling woozy.

Becca told us that the Bradley boy took her out in the fresh air, said he'd help her sober up a bit, then drive her home."

"I'm telling you," Howard Norman's voice was fraught with sarcasm and anger, "the boy was drinking and driving with no fear of getting arrested because of who his daddy is."

"Kyle took her outside, got her in his vehicle, and raped her there," Elaine continued. "She tried to stop him but could not."

"Did you file a complaint with the police?" Brett said.

"Went to Chief Warrenton," Howard said. "The man has since retired. He listened, then brought in Kyle's daddy. Next thing you know, Dan Bradley says they have a list of young boys at the high school willing to testify they all had sexual relations with Becca. She was fourteen-years-old, just a child. Swears she never had sex with anyone before Kyle took advantage of her that night. Anyway, Chief Warrenton sits us down and tells us that it would be totally humiliating for Becca if all these boys came forward like they said they would. He told us that in the condition our daughter was in on the night in question, she might not even be sure what she did or didn't do to encourage a young boy battling against his testosterone. He suggested that for Becca's own sake and reputation we let the whole matter go."

Elaine hung her head. She folded her hands on her lap to keep them from shaking.

"Howard, well, he wanted to wring all of their necks," Elaine said. "I was the one who convinced him to back off. I kept telling him that our daughter's welfare was the primary issue, even though I agreed that we were all being railroaded by a bunch of people with badges and the power to generate a cover-up for Kyle Bradley."

Elaine paused. She stared down at her empty hands, as her posture stooped. Tears began to fill her eyes and gently roll down her cheeks.

"Maybe I was wrong, especially when you consider that Kyle Bradley and everyone who covered for him have gotten away with everything. The only ones to suffer are Becca, Howard, and me."

Howard moved closer to his wife and put his arm around her.

"No. You were right, my love. We never had a chance fighting against those people. At least, we got our daughter and ourselves away from all of that mess."

Howard turned towards Brett and Roger.

"My job was already remote where I had regular clients within a geographical area that included portions of Florida, Alabama, and Tennessee," Howard said. "I only reported into our corporate headquarters in Tallahassee for a monthly meeting and on a few special occasions. So, moving to Crestview was something we could do with no problem."

"When our worst fears were realized," Elaine said, " and we learned that Becca was pregnant, we home schooled her during her pregnancy. Christopher is sleeping right now."

Once again, Elaine noted the surprised look on the faces of the two men.

"Becca originally agreed to give the baby up for adoption," Howard said. "We went through the whole deal with social services about the process for giving up a baby."

"The closer it came to the baby being born," Elaine said, "the more Becca began to have doubts. I told Howard that our daughter had been through enough trauma as it was. We should at least consider whether keeping the child was even feasible. I was no longer working and could take care of a baby full time."

"Do Dan Bradley and Kyle know that there's a little boy here who is Dan's grandchild and Kyle's son?" Roger asked.

"We're not sure about that," Howard Norman said. "We certainly haven't had any contact with them. I wanted to make them pay child support, but, once again, that raised issues as to whether we even wanted any of them involved in Becca's and Christopher's lives."

"To be honest with you," Elaine said, "we love Christopher. I bear the brunt of caring for him the most with Becca in school, but she adores the little guy and never hesitates to change a diaper, feed him, or do whatever else is needed."

"Dan Bradley used his position as the chief detective and his connections with people of influence and power to cover up a crime committed by his son," Howard said. "I'm telling you—Becca was raped by that boy and he got away with it."

"We heard from neighbors we knew back in Tallahassee," Elaine said, "that Becca was likely not Kyle's only victim. But, no matter what, he hides behind his father's badge."

෴

"You're awfully quiet," Roger said, as he and Brett were driving back to Tallahassee.

Brett's hands were tightly gripped on the steering wheel. His jaw was clenched.

"I don't like what I'm thinking, Rog. The Chief Detective has a son he's been covering up for over some time now. When a few girls in the same school as the Bradley boy are murdered, Kyle Bradley disappears. And his parents don't seem to be all that concerned."

"Which would be the case," Roger said, "if they know where their son is."

"Exactly," Brett said. "Like maybe papa decides it would be better to get the kid away from where all the action is. Then, Dan Bradley happens upon Chuck Richardson—a tailor-made suspect who is mentally-challenged and has a questionable past."

Roger nodded his head.

"And works at the very school where the victims come from," Roger added. "So, Dan Bradley locks in on Chuck Richardson to a point where he is blocking his top detective from considering any alternative to Richardson."

"Yeah," Brett added, "and is able to get the District Attorney on board, either as part of a conspiracy or simply because District Attorney William Farragut needs to prevail in this big case to bolster his political ambitions."

Brett pulled the car into a strip mall parking lot. He turned his body towards Roger.

"This is all conjecture, Rog, but if we're right, our jobs just got a whole lot more difficult. If Dan Bradley removed his son from the area because he knows or suspects the boy may be involved in these murders, we have barriers that will be incredibly difficult to get past."

Roger Clark nodded his head, then stared off in the distance.

"Yeah," Roger said, "big-time barriers named Dan Bradley, William Farragut, and Detective Wilson Jones."

CHAPTER TWENTY-FOUR

The Missing Boy

"How about you drop me off at Fulbright," Roger said as he and Brett were drawing closer to Tallahassee. "Let me see what I can glean from somebody inside. Better that I do this relying upon my role as an investigator. If you drive away, park somewhere a few blocks from the school, I'll signal you when I'm back outside."

When they reached the school, Roger quickly exited the car and walked into the building. He spotted the door marked as the office of the principal and walked in. The room he entered served as the receptionist's station and a waiting room. The name plaque on the woman's desk identified her as Marianne Hurley. There were several chairs lined up along a side wall.

Roger introduced himself and handed Hurley one of his business cards. He explained that he was an investigator working with Brett Gatlin, the defense attorney representing the man charged with murdering the young girls from this high school. He told the woman that he was seeking information on the whereabouts of Kyle Bradley.

The woman wore her gray hair in a bun. Her reading glasses were attached to a chain that hung around her neck. As she looked up at Roger, her smile was tight, and her eye contact was limited.

"Please have a seat, Mister Clark. I'll inform Principal Kenworth that you're here."

Hurley tapped lightly on the door to Kenworth's office and entered.

"There's a Mister Roger Clark here to see you, sir. He's waiting outside your office."

Marianne Hurley mentioned that Roger was a licensed private investigator. She never mentioned the reason why Roger wanted to talk to the school principal.

‌ℬ

Martin Kenworth walked out to the waiting room. He often thought about parents who sat in that room waiting for him to meet with them and explain why their child was being suspended, expelled, or, even worse, turned over to the police. The students called Kenworth "The Hammer" because of the way he handled disciplinary matters. He had no idea why a private investigator wanted to talk with him. Kenworth figured he'd know soon enough.

"You wish to meet with me?" he said as he did a quick study of Roger Clark.

Roger stood, extended his hand in greeting, introduced himself, and handed one of his business cards to Kenworth.

"I'm an investigator working with a defense attorney by the name of Brett Gatlin. I was wondering if I might have a few minutes of your time, sir."

"Step into my office," Kenworth said, as he abruptly turned around and walked in ahead of Roger.

The principal sat down behind his desk. Roger took a seat facing the man. Kenworth stared at Roger's business card and spoke without looking at his guest.

"So, what can I do for you, Mister Clark?"

"We are trying to get in touch with one of your students, a young man by the name of Kyle Bradley. It is our understanding that he has been absent from school for an extended time. I was wondering whether you might have information as to where this young man might be."

Roger watched as Kenworth's face turned pale. The principal opened his hand and let Roger's card drop onto the desk. He lifted his head and made eye contact with Roger.

"The young man you referred to has an authorized absence based upon parental permission. This is in addition to the fact that he, at eighteen, is of lawful age to leave school, if he so desires. His location is information I do not have and, if I did, I would not be at liberty to share that with you. I suggest that if you want to know where the young man is, you should ask his parents."

Kenworth picked up Roger's card, placed it in the top drawer of his desk, then looked back at Roger.

"Will there be anything else, Mister Clark?"

Roger understood Kenworth's words to mean that if Roger didn't have anything additional, it was time for him to leave.

"No, sir," Roger said. Then, he shook hands with Martin Kenworth, turned away, and left the room.

∽

"They finished searching the room. They carried out a few things, but I couldn't quite make out what they took. One item looked like Chuck's gym bag that he took to work every day. He'd put a few things in it like an extra shirt, some toiletries, and the lunch I'd make for him. Like I said, I couldn't see just what they took out of there and they never said a word to me. I was told that the police would make an inventory list."

Jocelyn McAllister was speaking by phone with Brett.

"Okay, well, don't worry about anything, Jocelyn. I'm on my way back to Tallahassee. When I get there, I'm going to visit with Chuck."

Brett could hear the sigh that emanated from Jocelyn.

"Oh, I am so happy to hear that Brett. Thank you."

∽

He made the call from his cell phone when he was in his car. It was highly unlikely that anyone would hear him if he spoke on his office phone, but he wasn't going to take any chances.

"Look, like I told you, the guy's name is Roger Clark, he's a licensed PI who works with Attorney Gatlin," Kenworth said.

"Yeah, I know who Clark is. He does all the investigative work for Brett Gatlin. What I want to know is what he wants from my boy."

"I don't know what he wants," Kenworth said. "He just said that they were trying to get in touch with Kyle. I didn't think it was a good idea for me to start asking questions about what he wants. In fact, I pretty much blew the guy off and told him that if he wants to know more, he should contact you. I didn't want this guy to think that I had any particular interest in anything related to your son."

"Okay, okay. You did good, Marty. Just keep your eyes and ears open and let me know right away if you hear anything more."

He hung up the phone from Kenworth. He didn't like this—didn't like it at all. He needed to remain alert and find ways to stop Clark and Gatlin from finding out anything more.

Martin Kenworth's hands were shaking when he placed his cell phone down on the passenger seat. This was something that he hadn't anticipated. He hoped that Bradley could take care of this.

‿

When he was back in the car with Brett, Roger spoke about his encounter with Fulbright High School's principal.

"Initially, I thought the guy just might be hardened from the rigors of his job and dealing, so often, with negative issues. I also considered that educators tend to be very careful when it comes to anything having to do with someone else's kids. But, by the time I left, I was convinced there was more to this story."

Brett turned momentarily towards Roger and spotted his wrinkled brow and set jaw. Roger's head was tilted as he mentally weighed all that he had seen and heard.

"I'm all ears, Rog, tell me what's on your mind."

"You know, I don't ever want to go on impressions and hunches when I'm reporting on something with you. I promised you when I agreed to work with you that I'd always relay info for which I have supportive facts. That's what you need and deserve. Hunches and someone's inner gut won't stand up in a court of law."

"I appreciate that, man. It, along with the confidence I personally have in you, makes everything and anything you tell me something I can trust. And we both agreed when we started working together that things may change from our initial thoughts and impressions, but we've got to start somewhere. And when something we initially believe to be true ends up being disproved, we've made some progress even then."

Roger smiled and nodded his head. Roger Clark was not one to draw too close to anyone nor put a great deal of confidnce or trust in another person. As Roger often said in times past, "When I was alone in the cockpit of the most incredible fighter jet ever created, no one else was with me for me to rely upon. Every decision, major or small, was mine. I quickly learned that the only person I could ever fully trust or turn to at times like that was myself."

But, Brett Gatlin was different and he and Roger had already forged a mutual trust that defied both of their normal personal habits.

"Thanks, Brett. Like I say, I can't exactly say why, but I had the feeling that Martin Kenworth was lying to me. Something inside me says that Kenworth is linked closely with Chief Detective Bradley and knows exactly where the Bradley kid is right now."

"And, if true, then Kenworth would likely know why Bradley pulled the boy from school," Brett said.

"Bingo!" Roger said. "Kenworth's got two, possibly three young girls who attended his school murdered and I didn't see a man willing to do anything to find out who may have killed them—as crazy as that sounds."

Gatlin waved his right hand dismissively.

"Maybe there's no need to expend a whole lot of thought and energy in solving something you already know—especially when you have someone locked up and ready to take the hit for a crime he didn't commit.

You talked about hunches and impressions a moment ago. Well, I have a bad feeling about this entire thing. I'm thinking we may have a young man hidden away somewhere who just might be a murderer."

CHAPTER TWENTY-FIVE

A Major Coverup

Brett headed over to the jail. He was able to have Chuck brought out of his cell to a small room. Although Chuck had his hands cuffed and wore leg irons, Brett hoped that being out of his cell might serve to lift Chuck's spirits.

"Are you gonna get me outta here?" Chuck said. "I mean, ain't that what lawyers do?"

Brett smiled, reached over, and tapped Chuck's arm.

"I did file a motion with the court to see if I can get the judge to set bail and let you leave this place. But, I want to be honest with you. It's not going to be easy to get a judge to agree in any case that involves multiple homicides."

Brett immediately spotted the confused look on Chuck's face.

"In some cases, Chuck, a judge makes you put up money and you get out of jail until a trial is held in court. And if a person runs away, they lose all that money. But when someone is charged with murder, especially with killing more than one person, it's really hard to get a judge to let that person out of jail."

"But I didn't kill anybody," Chuck said. "How can they make me stay in here when I never killed nobody?"

"I know you are innocent, Chuck, and that's what we're going to prove. But, for now, you just have to be patient. These things take time. I just need you to stay calm."

As Brett walked away, he remained concerned about Chuck. The man was so unstable and unpredictable. Every minute of his presence in jail was like a detonator marking off time until the explosion occurs.

∽

Roger called Wilson Jones and the two men agreed to meet at a coffee shop on the other side of town from the police station. Detective Wilson Jones was shaking his head. His eyes bore an incredulous stare as he sat in silence with Roger Clark. Jones felt a tingling in his skin, while his heartbeat raced. He said he would remain open to the possibility that Charles Richardson was not guilty. He agreed that he would follow up on justifiable leads provided to him by Brett and Roger. He promised himself that despite the fact that he was placing his job in jeopardy, he would pursue the truth and prioritize integrity over all else.

But, he never expected this!

"You gotta be kidding me, Clark. You're telling me that you and Gatlin suspect that Dan Bradley's son might be behind these recent murders and that Dan and some others might be involved in a conspiracy to cover up what Kyle Bradley has done? Is that what you want me to believe? Dear God, do you realize the implications attached to what you're saying? Do you have any idea what will happen if you are totally wrong?

Dan Bradley is not only the Tallahassee PD chief detective. The man is well-connected throughout this city. Your boss is putting his license to practice law at stake."

Jones paused for a moment, hung his head, then muttered words that sent a chill through Roger's body.

"Besides, do you realize what they'd do to stop us if you're right?"

Roger stared directly into the detective's eyes. He shrugged his shoulders, then lifted a hand with its palm facing Jones.

"When we all agreed to dig deeper into why Bradley was hindering the investigation into the murders of these girls, we had no idea where the evidence would lead us. You of all people know," Roger said, "that criminal investigative work isn't a perfect science. You work off of hunches and limited info. You test the waters to determine whether something has any real substance to it.

We went into this thing only knowing that you've got a supervisor who's doing everything in his power to stop you or anyone else from looking beyond Chuck Richardson. In fact, he's consumed with ending the investigation now."

Wilson Jones was slowly nodding his head. His hands were curled into fists and his lips were shut tight.

"You can't possibly think," Roger said, "that Brett and I didn't already believe that Bradley's actions were troubling to you and raised your suspicions some time ago."

"Yeah," Jones said, in what was a whisper, "I've been knowing that there had to be something deeper, something personal motivating Dan. But, hell, this is a damn powder keg.

If Bradley is letting another man take the rap for something that he either knows or suspects his son is responsible for, well, need I tell you that this changes everything? And if it's true that others may be involved with him... "

"We've got a criminal conspiracy," Roger said finishing Jone's statement, "and it's gonna blow up in all of our faces."

Roger reached out and slapped the palm of his hand on the table.

"Detective Jones, it's time for you to reveal your hand. Where are you in this? I know there's a part of you that probably thinks that you have the most to lose, but, you're wrong. Like we've said before. we've got a man sitting in a jail cell with everything geared towards convicting him of multiple homicides. The people lined up against him—people like Dan Bradley and District Attorney William Farragut—are a whole lot more powerful than you, me, and Brett Gatlin.

And let me tell you something, Wilson, I know Brett Gatlin a whole lot better than you do. Gatlin will absolutely never back down on this, no matter what's at stake. Brett is not only my best friend, he's someone I deeply respect and admire.

You can do whatever you choose, Jones, but this thing isn't going away, my friend. Don't look for a rug to see it swept under because that ain't gonna happen."

Jones looked up, stared back at Roger, and shook his head. His jaw was tight. He leaned his body forward and pointed a finger at Roger. The tension in the room was mounting. Jones moved his mouth to speak, then stopped. He opened his mouth again and spoke.

"Where am I in this? You want to know where I stand. That's a great question. How do I answer that? I have a wife

179

and a family. There's no way I can afford to lose my job. I've got fifteen years of solid experience in law enforcement, more than eight years as a detective, that would transfer to other cities—other police departments. But, once the word gets out that I turned on my own superior, I'm finished. We live under that unwritten blue code that you never report on a colleague's errors, misconducts, or crimes, including police brutality. Also, a charge of insubordination is yet another career destroyer.

I don't know, man. I don't know where I go from here. I don't know what I do. This is a road that I've never been down before."

Jones paused again. Roger sat silently.

"I guess the best way to answer your question is to say that if it's ever proven that I helped to convict a man who is later proven to be innocent, it'll be because I made an error in judgment based upon what I genuinely believed to be solid evidence. I'll never, under any circumstances, whatsoever, be a part of someone being railroaded."

Roger put a thumbs-up. Wilson Jones paused, took in a deep breath, then exhaled, before speaking again. His brow was furrowed. His nostrils were flared. His eyes were cold and flinty.

"But there's something else involved here. I don't like being played. I had Dan Bradley in my face, spittle spewing from his mouth, threatening me and my job, treating me like a delinquent kid in the principal's office. Warning me to stop investigating the murders of these young girls. He ordered me to concentrate on building a case against your client."

Wilson shook his head.

"Nobody treats me like that for whatever reason. So, I'm going to continue to work with you but, if I go after Bradley, I've got to know that I'm not just chasing shadows. The way things stand now, I don't know how far I go. I have too much to lose here—too much that I worked hard for over so many years. I can't make any promises or give you any guarantees. You asked where I stand, that's my answer. That's the best I have to offer. That's the best I've got to give."

∽

The sun had set when Brett walked out of the jail. The light that covered the area in the parking lot outside the jail where Brett parked was out. Brett neither saw nor heard the man who attacked him. The initial blow struck Brett on his neck behind his head and dropped him to the cement. He spotted two men wearing dark ski masks. One of them, a burly man who was about five feet eight inches tall, began to kick Brett in the ribs. Despite the pain and the wooziness from the initial blow, Brett spun his body away and made his move. He reached out, grabbed the man's ankle, and twisted. The man fell to the ground. Brett moved closer and threw punches to the man's head. He reached over attempting to remove the ski mask.

The second man, who was six feet two inches tall and had a thinner body frame, dropped to one knee, and placed the razor-sharp blade of his knife on Gatlin's throat.

"You make one more move Gatlin and it'll be your last one. Here's the deal. If you want to stay alive, get out of Tallahassee now. Stop sticking your nose in other people's business and messing with their families. Are we clear, Attorney Gatlin? This is not a suggestion. It's a warning—your last warning. You won't get another."

The man rose to his feet. Meanwhile, his burly friend, who was now standing nearby, kicked Brett several more times, including a kick to the side of Brett's face.

⁂

At the time that Gatlin was attacked, two men were poised, watching, waiting outside the coffee shop where Roger Clark was meeting with Wilson Jones. The man with the shaved head stood at six feet three inches and had a well-groomed goatee. His partner was an African-American who was six feet one and had a scar on his face that extended from his left cheek to the edge of his chin. Their bodies tightened when they spotted Roger exiting the shop. They pulled on their ski masks and moved slowly, cautiously closer to where Roger had parked his Jeep. They were ready to make their move when they spotted Wilson Jones walking out behind Roger.

"I'm out," the African-American stated. "I don't fool with no cops. All's I was told was that Clark was in this place. Nobody said nothing about a detective. I ain't messing up a cop."

"I hear you, man. I'm with you," the man with the shaved head said.

Then, the two men quietly slipped away and left the area.

CHAPTER TWENTY-SIX

They Mean Business

It took several minutes for Brett to get to his feet. His head ached, he was so dizzy he nearly lost his balance and fell. Within a minute or two, he began to vomit. Brett had seen his share of concussions among players when he was an all-state quarterback on his high school football team. He knew that in addition to several broken ribs, he had a concussion. He made his way to the driver's side door and climbed into the car. When he did, he struggled to maintain consciousness and knew he was not in position to drive. He leaned his head against the steering wheel and closed his eyes.

∽

Roger called Brett and reached his voicemail. He figured that Brett might still be in the jail with Chuck. He waited for about thirty minutes and called again. The phone rang several times before going to voicemail once again. He drove to the motel where he and Brett were staying and saw that Brett's car was not there. He called Brett's phone again and, once again, Brett did not answer.

"Where are you, bud," Roger muttered to himself. "You're beginning to worry me. What's going on? Answer your phone, bubba."

At one point in time, Brett heard his phone ringing and vibrating. He reached over, but he was so groggy, he only knocked the phone on the floor of the car where he could not reach it.

Roger called again several more times.

"Makes no sense you'd still be at the jail," Roger muttered, "unless something's gone wrong."

Roger grabbed the fob to his Jeep and headed to the jail to see if Brett's vehicle was still there.

∽

Chattahoochee is a city within Gadsen County, Florida, and located about forty miles northwest of Tallahassee. The city has its own police force with ten sworn officers. The police chief, Albert Marion, was a childhood friend of Dan Bradley.

The old white wood-framed farmhouse was in need of a paint job. The handrail on the steps leading up to the front porch was loose. But the building itself had withstood the ravages of weather and time quite well. It was situated outside the city on twenty acres of what was once a forty-acre tract.

The moment his father entered the kitchen, the boy, who was seated at a table, lifted his head and glared at him. He was not prone to be disrespectful to his dad, but this time he felt as if his father had gone too far.

"You had no business taking me out of school and hiding me away here at this piece of crap house."

"You watch your mouth, son. My grandparents lived in this house and farmed this land all of their adult life. I used to come here in the summers with my dad. This place has a lot of good memories for me.

I already told you that you need to stay out of sight until things calm down a bit. This is for your own good. So, calm down and take hold of your temper, boy. Maybe you can relax and enjoy your time out here with nature."

Dan Bradley chose this location to place his son, Kyle, while the murders of two, perhaps, three young girls from Kyle's school had everyone on edge.

"Enjoy myself with nature. Who you kidding, Dad? You got babysitters out here watching every move I make. Maybe you should just use a pair of your handcuffs and and hook me up to something where I can't move at all." Kyle said.

"I'm sorry, Kyle, I'm just trying to protect you is all. It's too bad that you're just not mature enough to realize that I have your best interests at heart."

Kyle laughed. He glowered at his father, then laughed aloud.

"Who you kidding, Pops? That's a joke, man. You're not interested in protecting me. All you care about is protecting yourself and your reputation. Gotta keep things clean if you're gonna run for state rep. Having a wayward son around could cost you an election."

The loud cracking sound of Bradley slapping Kyle across his face interrupted the words being exchanged between father and son.

"I'm warning you. Think what you want, Kyle. Just make sure you stay put and do whatever you're told. I'm the only reason you're not already in jail on drug charges and more. I've been following behind you cleaning up one mess after another. Are you forgetting that it was me who helped when you were charged with rape and ended up getting that young girl pregnant. And now we got us several girls from your school who were abducted and... "

"I already told you. I've had nothing to do with them girls. Nothing. Zero. You're crazy trying to pin something like that on me."

Dan Bradley said nothing in response to his son. He regarded Kyle to be a notorious liar who perfected those skills over the years. As far as Dan was concerned, he made up his mind to never believe a word the kid said. Hell, he was not the only one who suspected that Kyle might have something to do with the girls who'd been murdered. They'd not been raped, but Kyle might have tried or, perhaps, he was simply making them pay for past rejections.

A spotlight on Kyle Bradley might expose a few others who helped coverup the boy's misdeeds in times past.

"I don't have time to argue with you, Kyle. I put you here and you'll stay put until I feel things have calmed down and otherwise been taken care of."

Bradley made sure that the men he'd hired to stay with Kyle on this property and keep him in check had all that they needed.

❦

Roger spotted Brett's car, drove over to it, and found Brett. He quickly got Brett into his Jeep and raced to the hospital emergency room. While the doctor on duty tended to Brett, Roger called Detective Jones.

"Preliminarily, they're saying a concussion and some broken ribs," Roger said. Based upon what they said, they should be doing some x-rays right about now and may even do an MRI. They believe he was initially struck behind the head with some type of blunt instrument."

"Have you been able to talk with him?" Jones said.

"No, not yet. Even when I drove him to the hospital, he was, at best, semiconscious. I tried speaking to him, but got nowhere."

"Okay, hold tight," Jones said. "I'm on my way over there."

While Brett was undergoing some tests, Roger made the call to Wireless.

"What, Brett was attacked?" Wireless said. "Is he gonna be alright? How bad is he hurt? Do we know who did it?"

"Hold on, Wireless. One step at a time. We'll know more soon after they finish with the x-rays and any other tests they've got in mind," Roger said. "He's been roughed up. No doubt about it. But, Brett doesn't go down easily and he sure as hell doesn't stay down.

Listen, man, I'm believing this has something to do with the fact that we've stirred up the natives with our interest in finding Kyle Bradley. We need you to escalate the search for this kid. I'll see what I can dredge up on my end to help, but we're not exactly dealing with people that have a strong desire to share any information with us."

"I'm on it," Wireless said. "Let me give this some additional thought and see if I maybe can come up with another angle."

"Great. Sounds good, Wireless. Appreciate whatever... "

"Hey, Roger," Wireless interrupted. "You'll keep me informed on Brett's condition?"

"You can count on it, Wireless. I'll get back to you as soon as I know more."

∽

The hospital wanted to keep Brett overnight for observation, since he had suffered a head injury.

"We'll be better positioned to monitor him throughout he night," one of the attending doctors said.

Roger and Wilson Jones waited until Brett was settled in a room before attempting to speak with him. Brett was groggy, but he was coherent.

"Can you tell us anything you remember?" Jones said.

"I was walking towards my vehicle when I was struck from behind. The force of the blow was strong. I fell to the ground," Brett said. "Everything after that was vague, like in a distant dream. There were two men. They wore dark ski masks, so I couldn't see their faces. One of them was around five feet eight and had a burly build. The other was taller. I'd say, six two and thin. The shorter guy began kicking me in the ribs. I was able to spin away from his feet, grab his ankle and twist. He fell to the ground and I remember reaching over trying to pull his mask off."

Brett was breathing heavy. His brow was covered with perspiration. Wilson Jones reached over and touched Roger's arm.

"Let's give him a moment to regroup," Jones said. "He's been through a lot."

Roger reached over for a cup and a pitcher of ice water left on the stand near Brett's bed by one of the nurses. He held the Styrofoam cup close to Brett's mouth, so he could sip water through the straw. Jones grabbed a small towel and wiped Brett's brow.

"Do you want to continue talking," Jones said, "or should we hold off for now?"

"Th-thanks," Brett said. "I'm okay."

Roger and Wilson waited in silence. Brett began to speak again.

"Before I could pull the mask off of the guy's face, the second man knelt down and pressed a knife against my throat. He was the only one who spoke. He gave me an old western warning and told me to leave town."

Brett chuckled at his own comment.

"Anyway, I took it that they were warning me to stay away from anything having to do with Bradley's kid. Then, the burly guy was back on his feet and he kicked me in the head, on the side of my face."

"Brett, I know things happened quickly and you were already hurt, but I've got one last question," Jones said. "Is it possible that either of these men was Dan Bradley?"

Brett never hesitated.

"No. The guy who kicked me was much stockier in his build than Bradley and the other man also did not fit Bradley's body build at all. Plus, his voice was different—more nasal sounding."

Roger stared over at Jones and without a word passing within them, Jones nodded in silent agreement.

"Okay. That's enough, Brett," Roger said. "You need to get some rest. There's no sense pushing yourself anymore tonight."

"One more thing," Brett said. "I remember now. As the burly guy stood over me that last time, I spotted what he was holding in his hand. It was one of those expandable black steel police batons."

CHAPTER TWENTY-SEVEN
In Search of the Killer

On the way back to his motel room from the hospital, Roger called Wireless and updated him on Brett's condition. Wireless was relieved to hear that Brett's injuries were not life-threatening. Also, he would not require any surgery and the prognosis for a full recovery was positive.

"Well, that's the biggest difference between Brett and me," Roger said. "I've been so hard-headed all my life, a blow to my skull probably would have broken the steel baton."

Wireless laughed aloud.

"I still haven't come up with anything that would help us locate Kyle Bradley," Wireless said. "But, I want you to know that I won't quit until I do."

"Hey," Roger said, "I've got all the confidence in the world in you, Einstein."

⁂

Brett wanted to contact Tara, but after his limited session with Roger and Wilson Jones, Brett was completely exhausted. Roger offered to call Tara and Brett agreed.

Tara was shocked to learn about the attack on Brett. She cried as they spoke.

"He's banged up pretty good," Roger said. "The blow to his head generating a concussion was the most signicant injury. But the doctors do expect he'll be okay. He just needs some rest."

Tara made it clear that she wanted to come to Florida right away—despite her work schedule. After some discussion and a few intermittent phone calls, Roger arranged things so that Addie would have Tara stay with her.

"She'll meet you at the airport and drive you to Tallahassee where Brett is hospitalized," Roger said in talking with Tara. "We'll make sure that you have access to see Brett. We don't know, at this point, how long he'll be in the hospital."

∾

The sun had barely risen and begun to bleed through a small opening in the window curtains when Roger opened his eyes the next morning. He was apprehensive, troubled by what he might learn as he punched in the number that he was given at the hospital to check on Brett's condition. After some eight or so minutes, a nurse came on the line.

"Mister Gatlin had a somewhat difficult night, Mister Clark, plus the team nurses regularly woke him. We watch closely for any additional indications permitting us to measure the extent of a patient's head injury. There was some more vomitting, his eyes are still not well-focused, but when we spoke with him at various intervals during the night, he was relatively coherent. As I'm sure you realize, the final call on whether a patient will be discharged is with a doctor, but between you and me, I'd say they will keep him here for a few more days."

As Roger disconnected from the call, he could not contain the smile that covered his face. The news about Brett was pretty much what he expected. He remained confident that his friend would fully recover soon. Addie would be at the airport to pick up Tara later this morning and drop her luggage off at Addie's apartment. Then the two women would make the two-and-a-half hour trek to Brett at the hospital in Tallahassee. Roger would meet them there. He could not help but believe that seeing Tara would be the best medication Brett could possibly receive. He pumped his fist in the air and tossed his cell phone over on the unused bed. His first order of business would be to make a cup of coffee followed by a shower.

∽

"What happened with Gatlin? Your guys were supposed to put some pressure on him, not almost kill the guy."

"C'mon, Dan, you know that cops sometimes have a tendency to cross the line. The adrenaline starts flowing and they end up applying too much force."

Dan Bradley was on the phone with Albert Marion, the Chattahoochee police chief.

"And what about Roger Clark? Why wasn't he given a warning?"

"Look," Marion said. "I've got off-duty cops rotating on staying with the boy at the farmhouse, even though they don't understand all that's involved here. And two of our guys took care of the lawyer when he came out of the jail. But, the two guys I had lined up for Clark recognized Wilson Jones as a detective—don't ask me how, but they did. And, even though Jones was not the target, they were concerned that he might become aware and get involved in trying to help Clark. I'm sorry, man, but that's where our guys draw the line. They refuse to be involved in messing with another cop."

Bradley said nothing. He was receiving excellent support from his friend, Albert, and didn't want to do anything that might cause the police chief to pull back. Besides, Albert Marion believed that he was helping Bradley protect his son from drug charges and an upcoming trial where Kyle could otherwise be implicated. Albert had no idea he was protecting someone who may have murdered several young girls.

∽

Roger was groomed and ready to head out when a call came through on his cell. He considered that it might be Wilson Jones, Wireless, or even Brett. But, when he answered, no one said a word on the other end.

"Hey, I said this is Roger. Can I help you?"

The voice that responded was hesitant, quiet, and halting. It was also female.

"Th-this… this… is Mister Clark? Roger Clark, the… uh… the private investigator?" the caller said.

Roger chose to react with a calmness in an effort to encourage the caller to respond.

"Yes, ma'am. That's correct. How can I help you today?"

The gap of silence seemed so long that Roger wondered if the caller had disconnected, but, when he glanced at the screen, he saw that the call was still active.

"I-I need to know s-something, Mister Clark. If I talk with you... I mean if I tell you something, can it remain just between you and me?"

"It depends upon the nature of what you tell me, but, if it's at all possible, I will keep our conversation confidential."

The woman hesitated again. Roger chose another tactic.

"Listen, you would not have called me if you didn't think that what you have to say is really important. You and I both know that. I can sense that making this call was particularly difficult for you. What say, now that you took that first step, you tell me what's on your mind? Are you in trouble or in any danger?"

"N-no trouble," the woman said, "but I could be in danger, you know, if he ever finds out that I called you."

"Hey," Roger said. "I'll do everything I possibly can to assure that no one who would harm you will ever find out that you have called me. You have my word on that."

"My name is Marianne Hurley." And the moment she said it, Roger knew who she was. "I am Principal Martin Kenworth's secretary at Fulbright High."

"Yes, I remember you, Miss Hurley. Please tell me what's on your mind."

"When you came here to the school to meet Principal Kenworth, I never told him why you wanted to see him. If I had, he would have refused to see you. He's real tight with Dan Bradley at the Tallahassee PD. There've been problems with Bradley's son, Kyle, in the past. I'm talking about drugs and sexual issues with girls at the school. Kenworth, Bradley, and a few others have worked behind the scenes to cover up for the boy. Kyle's a troubled child or at least he was. Even at an early age, the boy displayed emotional or behavioral problems. but his father didn't want to highlight the fact that he's got a boy with serious issues in his life."

Roger's attention was riveted on all that Marianne Hurley had to say.

"Miss Hurley, do you think Kyle had anything to do with Kelly Ann Lauren, Michelle Landry, and, maybe, Miriam Walton?" Roger said.

"I can't say for sure, but I'm convinced that his father suspects that he did. That's why he pulled the boy from school and has him hidden away. Kyle never formally withdrew from school. His teachers were told that he has some kind of illness and cannot be around the other students right now. They send him assignments so that he remains on schedule to graduate this year. Kenworth has told the teachers not to breathe a word about this or they could be in violation of HIPAA and subject to dismissal from their jobs, criminal charges, and subject to civil lawsuits."

"Miss Hurley, you stated earlier that Kyle is a troubled child or, at least, he was. What did you mean by that?"

"The boy has shown more stability of late. Not sure why, but it seemed to me that he was different this year, more mature. Then, next thing I know, his daddy pulled him from school."

"Do you know where Kyle is right now?" Roger asked.

"I do," Hurley said, "although I'm not supposed to know. And if Martin Kenworth and Dan Bradley ever learn that I've told anyone, there's no telling what they'll do to me."

CHAPTER TWENTY-EIGHT
Another Special Moment

Roger arranged to meet with Addie and Tara before they went to Brett's hospital room. He discussed his plan with Addie as she and Tara were driving to Tallahassee.

"There's a cafeteria on the first floor of the hospital. We can meet there, have some lunch together, and then Tara can go alone first to see Brett. As much as I'd love to see his face when he spots Tara, I think it's a special moment that Brett and Tara should have by themselves."

Addie laughed.

"My, my, for a tough fighter jet pilot, you can be quite romantic," Addie purred.

"Hmm, I'll show you some romance when we're together," Roger said causing both he and Addie to laugh.

∽

"The word I received is that Richardson's attorney, Brett Gatlin, was attacked last night. Couple of guys roughed him up. He's in the hospital with, at a minimum, a head injury and some broken ribs."

Wilson Jones was in Chief Detective Bradley's office telling him about the assault on Gatlin. Bradley was focused on some papers on his desk and did not bother to look up at Jones.

"They got any idea who attacked him and why?" Bradley said.

"No, nothing yet. No witnesses and police were not called to the scene," Jones said.

Jones was disgusted that his boss didn't even have the decency to stop whatever he was doing and make eye contact with his detective. He found it to be demeaning, but not inconsistent with Bradley' personality.

"Again, from what I've heard," Jones continued despite his negativity, "Gatlin's PI showed up at the scene and brought him straight to the ER."

Bradley finally lifted his head and looked at Detective Jones. He paused, shrugged, then spoke as if he were considering the possible answers to his own questions.

"You know," Bradley said, "it's possible some folks took exception to an attorney who would defend a murderer of young girls and decided to teach... uh... this sleazy lawyer a lesson. I don't need to tell you that we've got a lot of people very upset over these murders."

Jones did not respond, although he initially wanted to change Bradley' reference to Charles Richardson as being an alleged murderer. Bradley's theory regarding the identities of the attackers and their motives had some credibility, but Jones was not sold on its validity. Besides, Jones had since learned that the blunt instrument used to strike the back of Gatlin's head was likely a steel baton—much like the ones that police carry.

Jones had already ruled out the probability of the Siemens Street Gang being the ones who attacked Gatlin. The use of a steel baton did not necessarily establish that the police were involved, but Jones was having a difficult time fitting the pieces together.

∽

When Roger first saw Tara, he was initially at a loss for words. His mouth fell open and he shuffled back a step or two before quickly recovering and greeting Tara. Except for her hair color and the fact that she was an inch or so taller than Kerry had been, seeing Tara was like seeing Kerry alive again. Brett told Roger about the incredible similarity in appearance between the two sisters, but being face-to-face with Tara offset any advanced warning Roger may have received and served to take Roger's breath away. Brett was right when he said that seeing Tara was like seeing a ghost.

After the initial shock, Roger felt a warmth inside his body. He knew Brett well enough and trusted his friend to never use Tara as a substitute for Kerry. But he liked the fact that Tara was providing Brett with another opportunity to love again.

As Tara rode the elevator up to the floor of Brett's hospital room, she felt a churning in her stomach and a tingling in her arms and legs. Her breathing was accelerated. As she thought of what Brett had gone through and envisioned a steel rod slamming against the back of his head, Tara fought against the tears that were forming in her eyes. She dabbed her eyes with a tissue and stepped out of the elevator to head to Brett's room.

Vincent J. Sachar

The door was slightly ajar, Tara heard nothing emanating from within, so she slowly pushed the door open. She gasped when she spotted Brett. He was lying in the bed with his head slightly propped up on two pillows. Even from a distance she spotted the swelling on the right side of his face and the purple brusing around his right eye. She carefully approached the bed and smiled broadly when Brett opened his eyes and spotted her. His eyes appeared dazed, but the smile that covered his face made it clear that he was aware, conscious, and very pleased to see Tara standing over him.

"Hello, my darling," Tara whispered.

"Tara? What? You're here?" Brett said with his words only slightly slurred.

"Well, I just happened to be in the neighborhood, so I thought I'd drop in," Tara said with her captivating smile now accompanied with the crystal globules that detached from her eyes and rolled gently down her face.

She leaned over, Brett reached up and placed his arms around her neck, and the two lovers kissed deeply. It was the kind of kiss that attempts to make up for so much time not having been together. It was a kiss that emanated from two people mature enough, stable enough to have quickly settled the issue of how they feel about each other. It had all the sparks and chemistry of soul mates pouring out the contents within their hearts.

Tara and Brett stared into each others eyes, despite Tara's flowing tears and the tears that now filled Brett's eyes.

"I love you, Brett," Tara whispered.

"And I love you," Brett responded, as they kissed again. "And, yes, I know what you want to ask me and the answer is that I'm honestly okay. In fact, with you here, I'm much better than I was before I opened my eyes and saw you standing next to my bed. It took a moment for me to realize that I wasn't hallucinating," Brett said while cautious that he didn't laugh too hard.

They kissed again. Tara stepped back for a moment, reached for a chair, and pulled it close to the bed. She sat down and held Brett's hand. She placed her other hand on Brett's face.

"How in the world did you get here?," Brett asked "Did you fly into Talla... "

"She flew into Pensacola," Roger said, as he and Addie entered the room.

Brett was smiling as Addie leaned over and kissed his cheek on the left side of his face. Roger touched Brett's arm and smiled at his friend.

"I can't believe this," Brett said. "Thank you both for helping with Tara."

"Are you kidding?" Roger said. "If we hadn't agreed to help Tara, she probably would've walked here from Indiana to Florida. There was no stopping her."

Brett laughed then placed his hands on his rib cage in a feeble attempt to stem the pain.

"Guess the old saying that it only hurts when I laugh has some credibility to it," Brett said, as he laughed and felt the pain once again.

✑

Tara never left Brett's side. She stayed in Brett's hospital room throughout the night, sleeping on a recliner that was in the room. She stayed with Brett the following day.

"Addie helped to change my flight so that I depart from Tallahassee in the morning," Tara said. "I honestly don't want to leave, but I have no choice. It's a miracle that I was able to get this time off in order to come see you."

Brett reached out and took Tara's hand.

"I think this long-distance dating is going to get old real fast," Brett said. "It already has."

Tara leaned over and kissed Brett. He took her hand, placed it on his lips, and kissed it. He stared into her captivating emerald eyes and marveled at the fact that he had been given a second opportunity to share a love with this incredible woman.

CHAPTER TWENTY-NINE

A Plan of Action

Tara had been gone for two days when Brett received word that he would be discharged from the hospital. Roger and Wilson Jones were with Brett in his hospital room waiting for the nurses to complete the paperwork for Brett's discharge. Brett was propped up in his hospital bed looking far better now. Roger was telling him the details of his conversation with Marianne Hurley.

"Based upon what Marianne Hurley said, there's an old farmhouse situated on some acreage outside of the city limits of Chattahoochie," Roger said.

Roger had some follow-up insight from Wireless but he acted as if he was the one who uncovered the additional facts. He didn't want to even refer to a third-party with computer forensic skills in front of Wilson Jones.

"I did a little research but couldn't find any property in that area owned by Dan Bradley or his wife. Finally, I found something owned by a limited liability corporation entitled, *Nostalgia Unlimited, LLC.* Dan and his wife are the two principals in the corporation. We have every reason to believe that's where Kyle Bradley is currently hidden away."

"And if he is," Brett said, "it makes sense that Bradley would have someone else there with the boy making sure that he stays put."

"My thoughts exactly," Roger said.

"I'm familiar with the Chattahoochie area," Jones said. "You're talking about an area maybe forty to fifty miles northwest of here. I've done some hunting in that area. In fact, I know a guy, Sid Justine, who's on their police force. Sid didn't make the cut in trying to get on with the Tallahassee PD. I could give Sid a call. Maybe he can help. Gotta be careful, though. Dan Bradley has a friendship with the Chattahoochie police chief."

Wilson Jones left the hospital and headed over to the station for a meeting. Roger took the time to relay his recent conversation with Jones to Brett.

"Sounds to me," Gatlin said, "that we have to work with Wilson with the understanding that there are limits to what he is willing to do. Look, Rog, we can live with that. We have to. This entire situation with Bradley and his son sucks. But, for Chuck's sake, you and I will have to ride it through."

Roger was already shaking his head, shifting in his chair, and frowning. He stared at Brett and shrugged.

"I've got this terrible feeling that you're going to tell me that you want to come with me to check out that farmhouse. Man, you just got slammed in the head with a steel rod, you have several broken ribs, and, if you ask me, your eyes still look kind of funny—like a guy who's not fully clear inside his own head."

Brett laughed at Roger's comments.

"They're going to send me out of here with a rib belt and I have a flak jacket that I'll wear. My head is more than clear enough, Rog. I'll be perfectly okay. Besides, you of all people should know that I believe we've got to follow up looking for the Bradley kid and there's no way I'll ever agree to you going it alone."

A broad smile covered Brett's face.

"Now, is there anything else on the agenda you care to discuss, Investigator Clark?"

❧

The plan was set. Brett and Roger would make a quick trek back to Milton and Pensacola to pick up a few items, including Brett's flak jacket. Brett insisted that they stop at a military surplus store and purchase a flak jacket for Roger.

"I'm telling you that's a waste of money," Roger said. "I flew an F-22 badass Raptor at Mach two class and dealt with so many Gs pressing against my body, I'm not sure that I have much left inside of me. My ribs are probably all fused together into one piece."

Roger laughed. Brett laughed along with him. This time, his ribs did not hurt. The two men would head for Chattahoochee in the late afternoon and, depending upon what they find, would use the cover of night to enter the farmhouse in search for Kyle Bradley. As they drove back towards the Pensacola area, Brett called Wilson Jones and informed him of their plans. Jones thanked Brett for the call but made no commitment to assist.

When Brett disconnected from the call, he immediately sensed that Roger was upset.

"Hey, Rog, I know you're disappointed that Wilson backed out on us. I am too. But we need to keep things in perspective. He's already helped us more than we might have anticipated. The guy does have a lot to lose. He's in a tough spot."

Roger shook his head and muttered "no" a few times before saying what was on his mind.

"I'm sorry, Brett, but there's a whole lot more than a guy's job at stake here. What good is a job if you have to surrender your integrity and even inadvertently sit back while another man is being framed for crimes he didn't commit? Sorry, but I just don't see it, man. I've often wondered about something, Brett. When you were falsely accused and every law enforcement officer in the country had you in their sights to take you down, how many of them had doubts about your guilt but did nothing about it? It's easy to take a stand when it doesn't cost you anything. The genuine evidence of character is when a person puts everything on the line in order to do what's right."

Brett reached over and fist-bumped Roger.

"Well said, Rog. I know you're right, but most people just don't have that measure of conviction or integrity. At least I can say that the best two people in the country did come forward when my life was on the line. A reporter named Kerry Anderson and a beer-drinking ex-pilot I met at a bar in Norfolk. And, I'll never forget what both of you did for me."

∽

"He says that those guys will be headed out to the farmhouse where Kyle is located sometime today."

Dan Bradley was on the phone with Chattahoochee Police Chief Albert Marion. Upon hearing those words, a rush of adrenaline raced through Bradley's body creating a tingling followed by a sudden coldness. This changed everything. He had hoped that putting some pressure on Gatlin and Clark would cause these men to back down and just concentrate on defending Charles Richardson. He never intended to further confront these men. He didn't want to do any harm to them, but how could he not protect his own son? If Kyle were to be found guilty of murder, the boy's life was essentially over at the age of eighteen. Plus, once criminal investigators began delving into the boy's life, a number of good men, outstanding citizens, could end up in big trouble for their role in helping Dan cover up his son's past criminal acts.

Bradley checked his weapon, added a few extra clips in his pocket, and headed for the place that once only represented special times with his grandparents. In the past, he enjoyed delicious meals and baked goods prepared by grandma Nellie and times sitting on the front porch with his grandfather. Now, the farmhouse was a hideout for his wayward son.

What was happening was never supposed to occur. He had no idea how these men even learned where Kyle was hidden away. Bradley' mouth was dry, his heart was racing, and his hands shook as he drove towards the farmhouse.

⌘

The team followed up on the items confiscated during the lawful search of the room where Chuck Richardson was staying, Chuck's car, and his apartment. They had already run tests for fingerprints and anything else that might link Chuck to any of the deceased girls. So far, they found nothing.

One of the items the police had taken from Chuck's room in his sister's home was the little gym bag that Chuck brought to work each day. It contained a half-eaten sandwich, an apple, and an empty juice bottle from the lunches Jocelyn packed for her brother each day. A pair of work gloves provided no additional clues. Safety goggles, a small flashlight, a handkerchief, and a man's watch completed everything that was in there. Nothing contained in the gym bag was of any help in furthering the evidence that would be used in an attempt to convict Richardson.

CHAPTER THIRTY

At the Farmhouse

After Brett and Roger found the farmhouse and acreage, they parked a distance away where Roger's Jeep could not be seen from the house. They walked closer and initially hid themselves at a spot where they had a full view of the farmhouse.

"No guarantee we're going to see anything specific here," Gatlin said, "but we've got to start somewhere."

"I could go knock on the door and say I'm in the neighborhood selling Bibles or something," Roger said with a smile on his face.

"Great idea. Now, who wouldn't fall for that, huh?" Brett said, followed by a laugh.

The two men laughed together, before Roger's facial expressions changed. His lips were pressed together in a grimace. He shook his head softly. Roger turned towards Brett.

"How're you feeling, Bro? How's the head, the ribs? If this is too much, we can forego everything for now and do this another time."

Brett smiled. He reached over and patted Roger's shoulder and gave him a thumbs-up.

"Thanks, Rog. I appreciate your concern, but I'm okay. I really am."

"I just want you to be free to tell me if you start to feel… whoa, hold on," Roger said. "Somebody's coming."

A car pulled onto the property. The driver exited and entered the house. Shortly afterwards, a different man came out of the house, entered a pickup truck on the side of the building, and drove away.

"If I had to bet," Brett said, "I would say that guys are taking turns staying with the Bradley kid—assuming Kyle is in there."

"Sounds like a solid wager to me," Roger said.

Just then, Roger's phone began to signal that a call was coming in. Roger mouthed an apology to Brett, as he immediately turned off the sound. He set the phone to vibrate only and answered the call. The caller was Wireless.

"Excellent," Roger said. "Appreciate the insight, Amigo."

He disconnected from the call and turned directly towards Brett.

"That was our master spy. He dug into Verizon phone records, identified a family plan belonging to Dan Bradley, his wife, and his son, then narrowed his search to further identify which phone belonged to Kyle. Once he did that… "

"He could pinpoint the location of Kyle through his cell phone," Gatlin said, interrupting Roger midstream in his conversation.

"Bingo!" Roger said. "Bottom line is that Kyle is here in this farmhouse, or at least his phone is."

"Excellent," Gatlin said. "That leaves us with only one decision—whether we enter now or wait and enter under the cover of night?"

Roger reflected for a moment on the choice that Brett presented.

"Okay, here's my two-cents," Roger said. "Assuming there's only one guy in there plus the kid, we could overpower them pretty readily. But the new dude just arrived, so he might be more alert now then he will be once the sun goes down in the next hour-and-a-half or so. I'll tell you, *Kemosabe*, my vote is for a less alert bodyguard and the added protection of darkness."

"Yeah, I agree," Brett said. "Besides, we won't have a long wait."

⁓

Dan Bradley kept a watchful eye on the area outside the farmhouse. He saw no sign of Gatlin and Clark. He assumed that, by now, they were out there somewhere. His vehicle was hidden away so that Gatlin and Clark would not know that he was inside the house.

He had time to work a bit further on his strategy. Afterwards, he would say that he and his son were at this family estate in order to check on things and make a few minor repairs. He might even say that he and his wife were considering putting the place up for sale. Then, he would classify Gatlin and Clark as intruders whom he did not personally recognize when he shot them. He would take the position that he was a man protecting the life of his son, as well as his own life. Archie Rivers, the off-duty cop in the farmhouse with Dan and Kyle believed that Dan was keeping his son away from some gang members who were dealing in dope and had begun to lure Kyle in. He and the other off-duty cops had been told that Kyle agreed to turn state's evidence against the gang, which had put his life in jeopardy.

"Hey, Archie," Dan said, "this may be nothing more than a false alarm, but my guys back in Tallahassee just gave me a warning that we might have some company coming our way. I need you to cover the back of the house. I'll take the front. Like I said, this may be nothing more than a false alarm, but no sense taking any chances."

Archie nodded and headed towards the back of the house. Kyle Bradley jumped up from his chair at the kitchen table. His arms were flailing nervously as he approached his dad.

"Who's coming? What's this all about? Are we in danger?"

"Take it easy, Kyle," Dan Bradley said. "I've got things under control. You just need to sit your butt back down and stay calm, son."

"Calm? We're like sitting ducks here and you want me to stay calm? I already told you I didn't have anything to do with those girls. Why don't we just get out of this place before anyone gets here?"

Dan Bradley checked his weapon again.

"It's too late for that, Kyle. They're already out there somewhere. Like I told you, sit back down and remain calm. This'll all be over very soon."

Bradley set himself up again at the front of the house. The farmhouse windows were covered with old drapes. Bradley used a tiny gap to see outside. If Brett and Roger made any move before the sun set, he'd see them right away. If they waited until darkness, they'd still have to try and find a way to enter the farmhouse. That might even be better for everyone since Brett and Roger would be two men breaking and entering a house.

Either way, Bradley would be ready.

CHAPTER THIRTY-ONE

Two Down

Darkness draped the area. It was compounded by the fact that there were no lights within miles of this place and a cloud cover hid the moon. It was a perfect night for the two men to remain hidden as they approached the house.

"We go around back and find a way in from there," Gatlin said. "This is an old farmhouse. There's no way with these doors and windows I can't get us in."

"Hmm," Roger said, "makes me want to check the door and all the windows on my condo when I get back."

Brett chuckled.

"You forget. You gave me a key,"

Brett laughed along with Roger.

"Okay," Brett said, "we're packing and that guy in there with Kyle may have a weapon, also. We're going to have to be careful to make sure no one gets hurt."

The two men moved silently and swiftly towards the back of the house. They expected that the man inside with Kyle would be towards the front of the structure. Brett saw a back window that he chose as their point of entry. Archie Rivers didn't hear a sound as he remained poised near the back door.

Brett and Roger were inside the house within minutes. The window that Brett had chosen placed them in a small room that had a sink and had somewhere over the course of years been set up to handle a washer and dryer. The room was currently empty.

Brett used hand signals to tell Roger that he would step outside the room. As Brett stepped out, Sanders was about three feet away from him facing in the opposite direction. He whirled and turned to face Brett, but before Sanders could make a sound, Brett had him in a choke hold until the man passed out.

"Okay, got him," Brett whispered. "We should have clear sailing to Kyle Bradley now."

Brett and Roger moved silently towards the front of the house. They spotted Kyle sitting alone at a kitchen table.

"Kyle Bradley," Brett said, startling the young man as he and Roger stepped openly into the kitchen. "There's no need to be alarmed, son," Gatlin said. "We have no intention of harming you. We just want to talk with you."

Brett was over at the table standing next to Kyle. Roger was standing at the entrance to the kitchen. Neither man had their weapons drawn. Dan Bradley stepped out from a nook in the room where he had been blocked from view by an old piece of furniture that contained dishes, cups, saucers, and other pieces of glassware. He immediately fired his gun at Roger's head. Brett gasped as Roger fell to the floor.

"Don't even think of taking out a weapon, Gatlin. Now step away from my son. I don't want you that close to him when I do what I have to do."

Kyle started to shout at his father.

216

"No, Dad, no! What're you doing? Are you crazy? The man said he wouldn't hurt me. Stop. Don't do this. Don't... "

Kyle spotted his father's finger ready to pull the trigger. He jumped in front of Brett.

"Put the gun down, Dad. Don't do this."

The shot resounded and the bullet struck Kyle in the stomach. He fell to the floor. Gatlin immediately bent down to tend to the boy. He was torn between helping the boy and running to Roger, but he knew that he could not possibly get to Roger without being shot to death.

Bradley's face was contorted. His hands were trembling. He initially stood in place as one paralyzed. Then, he shook his head, stared over where Kyle had had leaped from his seat just a moment before. Tears poured from his eyes.

"No, dear God, no. Kyle, Kyle," Bradley was screaming as he raced towards his son. Gatlin was on his knees. He pulled off his shirt and pressed it hard against Kyle's wound in an effort to stem the flow of blood.

"You did this," Bradley screamed at Brett. "I'm gonna kill you. I'm gonna... "

The front door burst open and three uniformed men, with their weapons pointed at Bradley, entered. They were followed by another man dressed in plain clothes.

"Sheriff's Department," the first man screamed out. "Drop your weapon. Do it now."

Bradley turned towards the men. Instinctively, he dropped his weapon before he made the full turn and was facing them. When he was face-to-face with the three sheriff's deputies, he saw that they had their guns pointed directly at him. Bradley stared into the eyes of the closest man and grasped just how close he had come to being shot to death had he not dropped his weapon. When he spotted the man in plain clothes, Bradley's mouth fell open. He gasped.

"W-what are y-you?" Bradley stumbled with his words as he stared at Detective Jones.

A moan from Kyle brought Dan Bradley's attention back to the reality that his son was shot and bleeding profusely.

"We need medical help for the boy," Brett called over to Jones, "and for Roger, too. We've got another guy at the back of the house."

Wilson Jones called for a couple of ambulances. Then, he walked over to Dan Bradley, glanced at one of the deputies who nodded, before Jones cuffed the man.

Dan Bradley glared at Wilson Jones and hissed.

"You low-life scum. You traitor. You're finished Jones. I'll see that you are. I'll see that you never wear a badge again."

"The only thing you're gonna see," Jones said, "is the inside of a prison cell."

One of the deputies walked closer to Bradley and recited his Miranda Rights. Another deputy bent down to tend to Roger. The third deputy cautiously walked to the back of the house with his gun drawn. When he reached the back door, there was no sign of Archie Rivers.

✧

Roger was surrounded by several medical emergency personnel. Brett remained on the side permitting them to tend to his friend. Roger was conscious now, although he was in a stupor.

218

The med tech treating Roger gave his preliminary analysis.

"If you're a gambling man," he said to Roger, this might be a good time for you to buy a lottery ticket." He then turned towards Brett and spoke to him.

"The bullet grazed your friend's skull. A fraction of an inch one way and we'd have a complete miss—the other way and we'd be dealing with a totally different story here."

Within minutes, the Med Tech had Roger sitting up with his body rested against a kitchen wall. Brett knelt down on one knee next to Roger.

"Hey, there," Brett said softly. "I'm right here for you, Rog. Just take it easy."

Roger's eyes were cloudy and his speech was slurred, but he was coherent and smiling. He reached over and clasped Brett's arm.

"Well... you know... I... uh... just didn't think it... right... for you to be the only one with... a head injury," Roger said. Then, he chuckled and it reminded Brett just how special a person he had as a best friend.

"This was all just too close for comfort," Brett said. "I don't ever want to play it this close again. I'm sorry, Rog, that you were put in such a precarious... "

Roger's mind was clearer now. His speech was not so halting.

"Whoa, Brett... hold on. Don't start that stuff again, man. Like I told you, man, I'm a big boy. You're not responsible for me."

Roger paused for a moment, took a deep breath, and continued speaking.

"I'm in this thing with you—always will be."

Brett smiled and clasped Roger's hand.

"Okay, man, I hear you."

"But... "

And, now, Brett was comforted when he saw a smile on Roger's face.

"Must say, Gatlin, I had no idea that working with an attorney could be so dangerous," His eyes were still cloudy. His head ached. But, Roger's smile sent a message that he

would be all right.

⁂

Roger and Kyle Bradley were both transported to the Capital Regional Medical Center in Tallahassee. Kyle's condition was initially listed as critical, but stable. Roger was listed in serious, but stable, condition. Kyle lost a lot of blood, but a preliminary diagnosis was that the bullet had not struck any vital organs. The bullet was lodged in the abdomen, however, and would have to be surgically removed. A call was made from the ambulance to put a team on notice back at the hospital.

The Gadsden County Sheriff's Department had the arresting authority over Dan Bradley. They made a decision to keep the man cuffed and under guard, but permit him to be at the hospital. Kyle's mother was contacted and she and her sister, Kyle's Aunt Trudy, came to Capital Regional. Brett drove directly to the hospital. Wilson Jones did the same.

Brett stayed late into the night in Roger's room. They chatted for a long time, which was helpful since initially the doctors wanted Roger awake because of his head injury. Then, when Roger fell asleep, Brett sat and read. Eventually, he headed over to his motel room.

It was a late night for everyone associated with Kyle Bradley. The ER doctors were able to stem the bloodflow. Then, after a quick series of tests to confirm what the doctors suspected, Kyle underwent surgery to remove the bullet and repair anything torn within his abdomen. There were no complications and the doctors proclaimed they were confident that this young man would make a full recovery.

Dan Bradley was distraught, finding it hard to believe that he had shot his own son and that his arrest would destroy his career and future ambitions. Once the surgery was over and the doctors spoke to Bradley and his wife, Dan Bradley was taken to the Gadsden County Sheriff Department Headquarters in Quincy, Florida where he was formally booked and charged with two counts of attempted murder.

Bradley called Lew Wilkes, one of the top criminal lawyers in Florida to represent him. Wilkes agreed to come to the sheriff's department headquarters despite the late hour. As a result, there would be no interrogations until Wilkes arrived. In the past, Dan Bradley pushed a few buttons and all issues disappeared. That would not be the case this time.

CHAPTER THIRTY-TWO

Case Solved

Brett Gatlin had never before seen the media overwhelmed by too much occurring at the same time. The news that a new suspect was being questioned in the murders of the Fulbright High School students merged with the shocking account that one of the most decorated members of the Tallahassee PD and a man anticipated to run for the state legislature had been arrested and charged with a double count of attempted murder.

There were reporters camped outside the jail in Quincy where Dan Bradley had been kept overnight. Lew Wilkes would begin his quest to get his client freed on bail following Dan Bradley's arraignment. Bradley would enter a plea of not guilty.

There was also a contingent of the media outside the Capital Regional Medical Center interested in the condition of Kyle Bradley and outside the Sheriff Department headquarters. Reporters were hopeful they could dredge up more with regard to why Kyle Bradley was being questioned in the murders of the Fulbright students.

There were also reporters on the hunt for Brett Gatlin interested in what impact, if any, the news concerning Kyle would have on Gatlin's client and whether Charles Richardson would be released from jail anytime soon. When Brett spoke with Jocelyn McAllister and filled her in on the latest developments, Jocelyn sobbed at the news that her brother might soon be freed.

"I'm not rejoicing someone else's misfortune," Jocelyn said after she composed herself, "but, an innocent man being freed because the guilty person has been identified is justice."

"We may need to hold off before we tell Chuck about this. I'm not sure he'll fully understand it all and we need to remember that nothing definite has been proven yet with Kyle Bradley," Brett said.

"Do you think the boy's guilty, Brett? Will they have enough on this kid to feel comfortable letting Chuck go?"

Brett lifted both hands in the air and shrugged.

"As a defense attorney, I'm cautiously optimistic, Jocelyn. You've got some within the police department who are confident they've got their killer. His father hid the boy away because he, an experienced detective, was convinced his son was guilty. I just learned from Detective Jones that they have now learned that Kyle Bradley was the last person known to be with Michelle Landry on the night she was killed. I don't have all the details on that yet, but that is a new and major development in this case.

So, yes, we have reason to feel good about the prospect of your brother being released. We just have to wait a bit and let the police talk with Kyle Bradley, which they've not been able to do because of his medical condition.

Kyle, at eighteen years old, was in a position to make his own decisions regarding his defense. He had his mother contact Billi Jo Webster, a young female attorney who handled a number of small drug cases for a few of Kyle's friends and classmates. His parents strongly objected to Kyle's choice of representation, but Kyle didn't care what they thought. Despite the fact that Billi Jo was nine years older than her client, she looked like a young girl about the same age as Kyle. Needless to say, this didn't serve well to bolster his parent's confidence that Kyle had made an appropriate choice.

Roger was released from the hospital and recovering well from his near-fatal shooting. He and Brett were temporarily back in Milton at the office when the call came in from Wilson Jones. Brett put the detective on speaker as he and Roger sat in Brett's office.

"With all of this crazy activity," Brett said, "Rog and I have not had the opportunity to properly thank you for what you did in coming to our aid. A few seconds or so later and you'd likely be attending our funerals right about now."

"That's if a big-named detective like yourself would take the time to drive to the Pensacola/Milton area to attend a funeral," Roger said before chuckling.

"Oh, I don't know," Jones said. "Any possibility that a lunch would be served afterwards?"

The three men laughed together.

"You doing okay, Clark?" Jones continued.

"Yeah, thanks for asking, man. I'm as good as new, except for this bandage on my head that makes me look like a zombie or something," Roger said.

"Good to hear, Roger. That was a close call for sure."

"Hey, Wilson," Brett said, "we thought you weren't going to get that involved in anything having to do with your boss, the honorable Chief Detective Daniel Bradley. What made you change your mind?"

Jones paused. Brett and Roger could hear the man's sigh before he chose to speak again.

"Look, I was conflicted. No doubt about that. I was hoping I could stay hidden behind the scenes while you guys got everything worked out when it came to Dan Bradley and Kyle. I was already struggling with how far I'd go when I made that call to my contact on the Chattahoochie PD. The moment I mentioned Bradley, his son, the farmhouse, and the fact that you guys were both headed that way, my guy acknowledged that he knew all about Bradley hiding his son there. He mentioned that Chattahoochie police officers were being paid to work off-duty and stay at the farmhouse with Kyle. The only thing is my guy believed that they were protecting Kyle from some drug gang members that the boy had agreed to testify against."

"So, you knew that your guy would report everything you told him to his police chief."

"Exactly," Jones said. " And, in turn, the chief, who was known to be particularly close to Dan Bradley, would tell him that the two of you were headed to the farmhouse. I had inadvertently set you both up. I needed to get to you quickly. Only thing is I needed some help and needed people with police jurisdiction in that county. That's when I made the decision to contact Gadsden County Sheriff Wilbur Robinson."

"Well, all we can say is that we're thankful you came when you did," Roger said. "Although, at the time you did show up, I was somewhere in 'LaLa Land.' I sort of remember, as in a dream, you and a few deputies arriving."

"So, where do things stand now with Kyle Bradley and Dan Bradley?" Brett said.

"We'll be interrogating Kyle along with his attorney this afternoon. That session will be conducted in the afternoon at the hospital," Jones said. "At the moment, I'm confident that we have our killer and you'll be able to get your guy released and all charges dropped.

As to Dan Bradley, we're beginning to uncover a pattern of how he and a few others conspired together to bend the law to protect Dan's son from past indiscretions. We have a team digging in now to see what, if anything, in his past actions might constitute a crime. At the same time, we'll be looking to see who else might be culpable for their actions."

"Where does District Attorney Farragut fit into all this stuff with Dan and Kyle Bradley?" Brett asked.

"Don't know," Wilson said. "Might simply be a case of an overly-zealous DA wanting to stick another feather in his cap by pushing through on Chuck Richardson before exhausting an investigation of all other potential suspects. We just don't know. Perhaps, we never will.

When are you two headed back to Tallahassee?"

"We plan on returning tomorrow," Brett said. "Rog gets his head checked today by his doctor in Pensacola."

"They can check my head any way they want to, as often as they want to," Roger said, "and I guarantee they'll come up empty. When it comes to my head, there's nothing there to be found."

Brett and Wilson Jones laughed.

❧

The "Father and Son Bradley Scandal" captivated the attention of the nation. National media personnel were present in Tallahassee. It was the primary topic being discussed on all the major news programs including panelists who engaged in discussions about the influence a father has on his children, the fact that power in law enforcement officials tends to corrupt, and questions as to whether a parent can ever forego their responsibility to protect their children and turn them in to the law.

CHAPTER THIRTY-THREE

We Have Our Killer

Following the interrogation session with Kyle Bradley, the Tallahassee Police Department and District Attorney William Farragut were comfortable with the statements they released at a press conference that was broadcast nationwide.

"The murders of innocent young high school girls has rightfully had our entire community on edge," Tallahassee Police Chief Morrison Tyler said. "I'm proud to say that our Department has diligently worked day and night in a concerted effort to identify and apprehend a killer whom we all feared would continually strike again until caught. Even though we had a primary suspect, we never stopped our exhaustive investigatory work," Tyler lied. "Today, we are relieved and breathe much more freely at the news that Kyle Bradley has been charged with these murders and is in the custody of the Tallahassee Police."

After commending the Tallahassee PD for their tireless efforts in identifying and arresting a suspect believed to be a multiple killer, District Attorney William Farragut addressed the issue of Kyle Bradley's age.

"There is no issue here. Kyle Bradley will be tried as an adult," Farragut announced. "He committed the crimes of an adult, so he will stand trial on that level. And let me assure you, we don't care at all who this young man's father is. The innocent girls he murdered had parents and family members, also. And they are entitled to justice and closure. We cannot bring their loved ones back, but we can assure that this young man will never again be in position to take another young girl away from her family and friends. Despite the youth of Kyle Bradley, this is not a time for sympathy, excuses, or justifications. Rather, it's a time to seek for justice to an extent and in such a way that the message is clear that heinous crimes such as these will never be tolerated and never be treated lightly in a society such as ours."

Kyle offered no verifiable alibis for each of the nights when Kelly Ann Lauren and Michelle Landry were abducted and murdered. He claimed to have no knowledge concerning Miriam Walton. He admitted that he was with Michelle Landry on the night she was murdered, but claimed that he brought her back to her house and drove away. His parents were out-of-town on that night and could not verify that he returned home at all. The police were able to establish that Kyle lied to them about where he was on the night Kelly Ann Lauren was murdered.

Following the press conference, Gatlin's petition for the release of Chuck Richardson was granted. Jocelyn was with Brett when Chuck walked out from the jail. She and Chuck wept in each other's arms. They both expressed their heartfelt gratitude to Brett Gatlin for the work he had done in fighting on Chuck's behalf.

"When you send your invoice to me," Jocelyn said before Brett left, "you can expect that I will add considerably to it. That will not only represent my gratitude for the above-and-beyond work you did for Chuck, but it will also help when you represent people less fortunate than us who desperately need, but are not able to afford, your services."

⁓

Brett and Roger were seated with Wilson Jones in his office. Each of them had a hot cup of coffee. Jones had already been named temporary chief detective, a position that everyone expected would be permanently his in the near future.

"We've had two witnesses come forward saying that on the night that Michelle Landry was abducted, she was with Kyle Bradley after she snuck out of her home. The two witnesses claim that Kyle, Michelle, and at least five others were smoking dope in a public park. Kyle claims that afterwards, he drove the girl back home. Could be he attempted to have sex with her and when she resisted, he killed her."

"I've never understood why we've never been told whether any of the victims were raped," Brett said.

"That's because none of the girls were raped. We've kept under wraps the fact that each of the girls had torn clothing evidencing that initial attempts to rape them were made. Could be these attempts were aborted and the killer, in a rage, chose murder instead."

Jones took another sip of his coffee.

"Well, now that your guy is off the hook, I guess you'll be headed back home?"

"Yes," Gatlin said. "There's no reason to hang around here any longer."

"Hey, Wilson," Roger said, "you once mentioned that you like to hunt. Do you fish?"

Jones smiled, made a gesture as if he were casting and reeling with a rod,

"I love fishing. If I had more time and knew some good locations, I'd be out there as often as possible."

"We've got some great fishing in our neck of the woods," Roger said. "If you do ever find some time, let me know and I'll take you to some of the best spots that I've already discovered."

"You know, I might just take you up on that," Jones said.

Then, he turned towards Brett and Roger in turn and extended his hand to each of them.

"I want you guys to know it's been a genuine pleasure working with you. You exposed me to things that taught me a lot about myself. Lessons I needed to learn by experiencing them—lessons having to do with personal integrity and reminding myself constantly why I wear a badge. You also helped provide a strong reminder that no matter how strong a case we seem to have against a suspect, our investigation should continue until all loose ends are tied up. If ever I can assist either of you, please don't hesitate."

Brett and Roger stood and walked out of the room, preparing to gather up their things at the motel and drive back home.

∽

"You know, it's hard to believe," Roger said, "that a young boy like Kyle Bradley could kill, not just once, not accidentally, but stalk, abduct, and then take his rage out on those girls."

Roger and Brett were on their way back to Pensacola and Milton.

"Let me tell you, Rog, I don't think anyone expected things to end up like this. But, you know, with a father that helped to cover up everything his son ever did, it kind of makes sense that Kyle would think that he could get away with anything."

Well, now he's gonna spend most of his life behind bars," Roger said, while shaking his head. "Such a shame."

"And I assure you, it's going to be a hell of a ride for his father, Dan Bradley. When a chief detective ends up in prison," Brett said, "well, let's just say that the stories you hear about things like that aren't pretty."

"Yeah," Roger said. "I agree with you, man. Plus, Dan Bradley ends up disgraced and stripped of everything—all that he's ever done for the good and all he's ever been—outside of prison and then finds his hell will continue big-time when he's behind bars."

"You know, Rog, I didn't have much time to reflect upon this back when I was falsely accused of being responsible for the lives of all those federal agents and Mexican federal police, but if I lived through that and ended up in prison... "

"Whoowee, Bubba," Roger said. "You're talking about a federal agent with those claims hanging over your head shut up in prison? Let's not even go there."

"At the moment," Brett said, "I could almost feel a small sense of pity for Dan and Kyle Bradley."

∽

She was in torment—the likes of which she'd never known before—even when she went through some trying times in the past. She could not control the weeping and sobbing. She found herself shivering and moaning and unable to eat since she first heard the news. Heard the news? Are you kidding? It seemed to be all the media was talking about. It was all that everyone was talking about.

She needed to come forward and tell what she knew. There was no question about that. She had to find a way to speak out. She would find a way. But, she was never so frightened in her entire life. The reactions of people close to her and close to him were beyond what she could imagine. They might take everything away from her. She was never so scared in her life.

Dear God, her body was trembling, the pain in her stomach was unbearable. Intermingled with her sobs, she found herself praying, begging God to help. Her sense of desperation was beyond anything she had ever before known or experienced.

CHAPTER THIRTY-FOUR

When Everything Changes

They showed up at the Tallahassee Police Department unannounced, without a scheduled appointment, looking for Chief Detective Wilson Jones. At least that was the name given to them as the man with whom they should speak. And they hit payday. Jones was in. And when the front desk informed the detective that a father, mother, and daughter with crucial information concerning Kyle Bradley wanted to see him, Jones readily agreed.

∽

Brett and Roger were on their way to Tallahassee following a call that Gatlin received from Detective Jones.

"All I know," Brett said, "is that Wilson said it was urgent and he wanted to talk with us before anything got out to the press. He said time is of the essence, so I agreed we'd come right away. Jones told me to exceed the speed limit. He said if we get stopped, put the state trooper straight through to his cell phone."

Brett shrugged and laughed.

"Sounds like serious stuff to me," Roger said. "Guess there's no sense speculating. We'll find out once we get there. Only problem is that whatever Jones has on his mind likely relates to Chuck Richardson or he wouldn't be calling us."

"Thought of that," Gatlin said. "Unless it has something to do with what happened at the farmhouse."

⌇

"Had a visit from the Norman family out of Crestview—Howard, Elaine Norman and their daughter, Rebecca," Wilson Jones stated. "I know you're both familiar with these folks."

"Yeah," Roger said. "We met with Howard and Elaine. Never did meet their daughter."

"She's a sweet young lady," Jones said, "although not quite as innocent as she may have seemed some time ago when she claimed she was raped by Kyle Bradley. The girl now admits that she and the Bradley boy had consensual sex one time prior to that night and her rape claims were spawned out of a personal backlash. Seems that Kyle told Rebecca that he thought it best if they stopped seeing one another."

"The old case of a girl being used and dumped?" Roger said.

"Actually, no. Rebecca claims that she later learned that Bradley actually had feelings for her, but he wanted to distance himself before he was forced to lure her into using drugs."

"I'm not sure that I'm following you on that," Brett said.

"Well, it seems Kyle was linked to a local drug dealer named Medford Smith, who, in turn got his supplies from... "

"From the West Siemens Gang," Roger said. "You recall that we're familiar with Smith and have you and your original unwillingness to investigate anyone beyond Chuck Richardson to thank for our encounters with West Siemens Gang members."

"Hey, Rog, give the beloved detective a break. He did come through when we needed him the most… uh… although you almost died in the interim and I had to fight some guys as big as those redwood trees everybody talks about."

Brett and Roger laughed. Jones fought hard against laughing.

"So glad to see that you guys are not prone to carry a grudge," Jones said as they all openly laughed.

"Anyway, excuse me for interrupting," Roger said. "I believe you were talking about the link between Kyle Bradley, Medford Smith, and the West Siemens Gang."

"Ah, yes," Jones said. "Kyle's job was to bring prospective candidates to Medford Smith. He was what they refer to as one of Smith's deputies. In return for what he did, Bradley received what they referred to as a cash commission and drugs for himself. And once Kyle got someone hooked, he was responsible to help keep that person coming. That's why he was with Michelle Landry on the night she died. Rebecca claims Kyle brought Michelle along with others to Smith to get her drugs, which he felt guilty about afterwards. Between Medford Smith and the West Siemens Gang, Bradley knew that he would be forced to get Rebecca Norman involved in drugs. "

"Okay, let me interrupt here for a moment," Brett said. "I'm getting the distinct impression that Becca Norman was speaking somewhat positively about Kyle Bradley. When we met with the Normans, we sensed the hatred they have towards that boy and his father. And, of course, we learned about the baby."

"Howard and Elaine Norman are extremely bitter towards Dan Bradley and, until now, they believed their daughter's claims to have been raped by Kyle," Wilson Jones said. "So, you can imagine just how difficult it was for Rebecca to admit that her rape accusations were bogus and the she has been seeing Kyle secretly behind her parents' backs. Guess the feelings those two kids have towards each other have some validity to them and the fact that they have a baby together has only strengthened things between them."

"So, what if anything about all of this is of concern to us?" Brett said.

"And had us breaking speed limits to get here today," Roger interjected.

"Bottom line," Jones said, "is that Rebecca Norman claims that she can support solid alibis for Kyle Norman on the nights that Kelly Ann Lauren and Michelle Landry were murdered."

Roger's mouth fell open and he slapped his hands against his cheeks. Brett stared off in the distance immediately pondering the impact this could have on Chuck Richardson.

"Hold on a sec," Brett said. "I thought you said that Kyle Bradley was with Michelle Landry on the night she was killed."

"Indeed, he was," Jones said. "Rebecca claims that after Kyle dropped Michelle off at home, he drove to Crestview. He took the money he got from Smith that night and gave it to Rebecca. In addition to Kyle wanting to assist with expenses related to the baby, seems Kyle and Rebecca were saving money together towards their future."

"Well, excuse me," Roger said, "but, who's to say the boy didn't kill Michelle before he headed to Crestview?"

"It's possible," Jones said. "There's no question that time is one of the most crucial factors to consider in a homicide case. It can strengthen the evidence against a suspect, shatter an alibi, or flat out eliminate a suspect. But, if Rebecca's testimony holds up regarding Kelly Ann Lauren, Kyle would have an alibi that is rock solid. Rebecca says that Kyle was with her that entire night when her parents were out-of-town attending the wedding of a relative in Kentucky. And we have always taken the position that the same person killed both girls.

I asked you both to come here before the media gets hold of this. News like this will create a media frenzy. They'll be exploring every aspect of this including the competency of me, our Department, and the DA. And, yes, we'll be back to square one. If Kyle Bradley isn't the killer, who is?"

"None of this automatically means that Chuck Richardson is the murderer," Brett said.

"No, of course, you're right about that," Wilson Jones said. "But Richardson was actually charged with the murders before all of this stuff with Kyle Bradley popped up. You know there will be people, even Bill Farragut himself, who will revert to the position that Richardson is guilty. The DA will apply his usual spin to everything, he'll mouth some jargon claiming it is better to have considered everyone and everything, especially when the evidence was strong against the Bradley kid.

If I were you, I'd anticipate immediate pressure being generated to arrest Richardson again. Needless to say, I wanted to give you as much warning as possible."

❧

The moment that Brett and Roger were back in the car, Brett turned to Roger.

"We need to contact Jocelyn and put her on notice. I'm thinking that we should head over to Jocelyn's house now. I believe I'll ask her if she is willing to take Chuck in again until we get past this next wave. This thing is going to be all over the news and reporters will be salivating for an opportunity to talk with Chuck. The very fact that the charges against Chuck were dropped when the focus shifted to Kyle Bradley is something we can use to our advantage if we ever go to trial. Shows how weak their position has been with regard to Chuck. But, keeping Chuck and Jocelyn calm should the authorities come after Chuck will be our biggest challenge.

❧

"They're going to come back after my brother again, won't they?" Jocelyn was weeping. In between her sobs, she made a strong attempt to communicate her fears and concerns. "They're gonna look bad enough with that whole Kyle Bradley fiasco. They're needing a quick fix and that means Chuck."

"They had Chuck in the spotlight as the killer," Brett said. "Then, they let him go, saying that Kyle Bradley was their guy. Stay calm, Jocelyn, and help me keep your brother calm. We've got a long way to go before they get a conviction on Chuck."

As Brett and Roger headed back home, Brett wondered just how quickly he would need to be back in Tallahassee.

CHAPTER THIRTY-FIVE

Move the Spotlight

The clock was pushing 7:30 p.m., but Wilson Jones was still at the station. He was seated alone in his office pondering what his next move would be. Kyle Bradley was not only likely to have his alibis stand proving he was not the killer they were seeking. The young man was also not the low-life they all thought him to be.

Kyle never sought his father's assistance in covering up anything he was accused of doing. In fact, he threatened to reveal to everyone that his father and others were actively covering up the rape accusation by raising false statements about Becca Norman. His father stopped him from doing so by threatening to have the baby taken away from Rebecca and her parents if Kyle so much as breathed a word to anyone.

Kyle was actively pulling away from Medford Smith and, hence, the West Siemens Gang, which was not an easy task. In the interim, Kyle made promises to Becca that he would never use any street drug other than marijuana. At the same time, he had already helped three of his customers to wean themselves of everything except weed. It was still not a perfect scenario, he was still dealing with something illegal, but he was taking steps in the right direction.

As Jones sat alone in his office drinking what might be his eighth cup of coffee for the day, his mind was focused on what he was facing now.

It's just a matter of time before it all comes out. Kyle Bradley remained silent, allowing himself to be in serious legal jeopardy, to protect the young girl he loved. Bradley never raped anyone. The kid's an honor student at Fulbright High and has been accepted to enroll in Florida State University next year. We not only don't have a killer, we don't have the monster we thought we did. It's time for me, time for all of us to accept the fact that Kyle Bradley is not our guy.

What do we do now? If we state that the murderer really is Chuck Richardson, we face the fact that we freed him and put him back out on the streets where he could have abducted and killed someone else's daughter?"

Jones was reading through everything and anything they had in their file regarding Richardson. He was on his third reading, looking at everything, anything that they might have missed. He read through everything related to the man's past— his misdemeanors, accusations made against him, medical and psychiatric reports, and analyses. There were things in Richardson's past that helped make him a viable candidate for homicide, but nothing, in and of itself, proved the man had killed anyone. Jones read through the interrogation sessions he had conducted with Richardson. By now, Jones was so familiar with everything he considered that he'd have to have a fresh set of eyes look over all this stuff.

For just a moment, Jones closed his eyes and tried to recreate the facial expressions Richardson made when he sat across from him in the interrogation room. He pictured the man's attorney, Brett Gatlin, sitting next to him, guarding his client from answering any questions that he should avoid. He pictured Richardson sitting there, sometimes with a look in his eyes that depicted the limited acumen the man had. He pictured...

That was when he saw it! Jones reached back into the stack of papers in the file that had been compiled, rustling though the papers until he found the statement given by Misty Lauren, Kelly Ann's mother. They asked Misty if anything was missing in the things that were found on Kelly Ann's person when her body was discovered. Misty mentioned that her daughter always wore a man's watch. It's face was too large for the young girl's wrist. The leather watchband bore two holes made with a sharp object to enable Kelly Ann to stretch the band tight enough for her to wear the watch.

"The watch had belonged to my late husband, Kelly Ann's daddy," Misty said. She wore it all the time, almost as if by doing so, she was still holding on to her daddy."

At the time, Misty said she would check at home to see if the watch was in Kelly Ann's room. Jones saw no record as to whether there was any follow up on that.

Meanwhile, Jones' fingers were racing through more of the pages and documents. It had to be there. He was sure he had seen it. Jones started again, moving a little slower this time, assuming he must have missed it on the first go-around. Then, he did find it.

The document was an inventory of items taken from Chuck Richardson's room under a lawful search warrant. Within that document there was a listing of everything contained in the little gym bag that Chuck brought to work each day. It contained a half-eaten sandwich, an apple, and an empty juice bottle from the lunches Jocelyn packed for her brother each day. There was a pair of work gloves, safety goggles, a small flashlight, a handkerchief, and a man's watch.

All of that seemed quite normal, except that when Jones sat across from Richardson and even afterwards when the man was arrested and put in jail, Jones remembered that Chuck was wearing a watch. It was actually an impressive timepiece with a thick silver metal watchband. The watch was a gift from Jocelyn to her brother.

Jones picked up the phone and punched in a number. She answered on the fifth ring.

"Mrs. Lauren, this is Detective Wilson Jones. Please forgive me for interrupting your evening, but something has come up in our investigation of ... uh... the abduction of your daughter, Kelly Ann. I was wondering if I could make a quick stop at your home. I could be there within fifteen or so minutes and won't need much time from you at all.

❧

Chuck Richardson was in his own apartment at 9:56 p.m. when Wilson Jones and two accompanying officers arrived, cuffed the man, read him his Miranda Rights, and brought him over to the police station. On the way to the station, Jones called Brett Gatlin to inform him of this latest development.

∽

"I don't care how late it is," Roger said, "I'm in. All I was doing anyway was sitting here watching some old Perry Mason episodes—which, by the way, is how I supplement my legal knowledge. I'm thinking that we could call Jocelyn while we're on the way. Then, if it's okay with her, you could drop me off at her place, while you're with Chuck at the station. That'll provide you with an opportunity to update Jocelyn when you come pick me up again."

"That sounds good, Rog. I'll head over to you now. Only question I have is… uh…Perry Mason? Really?"

"Well, I do watch that Matlock guy, also," Roger said, followed by a laugh that Brett joined in on.

∽

Roger didn't have any details to share with Jocelyn since neither he nor Brett knew why the police made such an aggressive move against Chuck.

"Brett will learn everything once he's at the police station," Roger said to Jocelyn. "What he'll do is spend some time preparing Chuck, then the two of them will sit with either Wilson Jones or some other police detective. When Brett is finished over there, he'll come here and update the two of us."

"I just don't know how my brother is going to react to all of this," Jocelyn said. "You know, he's not like you or me. There's no actual telling just how much he can comprehend and what goes through that mind of his."

244

"You should know by now, Jocelyn, that Brett will be very sensitive to Chuck and do everything he can to help to stabilize your brother. Chuck is in good hands."

∽

Brett didn't say much in the time he spent with Detective Jones. He listened carefully and thanked Jones for providing the insight that he did. Jones explained how he came about identifying that the watch found in Chuck's gym bag was worn by Kelly Ann Lauren on the night she was abducted and murdered. He told Brett that Misty Lauren identified it as her late husband's watch that Kelly Ann wore all the time.

"I had to pull some strings to take custody of the watch and get it out of the evidence room, so I could show it to Misty Lauren," Jones said. "Listen, Brett, I can't ignore the evidence that is staring us in the face. We've already got egg on our faces with this entire thing with Richardson. Yet, at the same time, by turning our attention to Kyle Bradley, we exposed his father for who the man is and what he's done. Plus, we already are onto Martin Kenworth and a local judge who were part of a conspiracy with Dan Bradley. But despite all of that, we just can't seem to escape from your guy."

"Why would Richardson keep a trophy from only one of the girls, not both?" Brett asked.

"Who knows why? Remember, Richardson is not your normal suspect. With his mental limitations, who knows why he might do or not do something. Maybe he just likes watches."

"I think you're jumping the gun on this, Wilson. You and your folks are going to look really foolish if the word gets out that you've arrested Chuck again and he's not the killer."

"We haven't formally arrested him yet," Jones said, ignoring the fact that they cuffed Chuck, read him his Miranda Rights, and did not give him a choice as to whether he would come to the police station. "But finding an item worn by the dead girl on the night she was abducted in your client's personal gym bag is compelling evidence."

Brett asked for the time he would need to explain things to his client before Brett and Chuck met, once again, with the detective in an interrogation room.

Brett worked hard to slow his own mind down and focus on Richardson. He needed to provide Chuck with a basic understanding of what was going on that would sustain Chuck for now. It was his responsibility to keep Chuck from panicking and doing something rash. He couldn't reveal everything to Chuck, because Chuck would not comprehend it all. He also was concerned that Chuck might talk too freely to others.

Other people would be shocked to learn that despite the fact that the police now had additional evidence that directly linked Chuck to the murder of Kelly Ann, Brett was more concerned with Chuck's well-being than with his criminal defense. Of course, that was made much easier the moment Brett realized that he knew who the real killer was.

CHAPTER THIRTY-SIX

Zeroing In

The news that Charles Richardson was once again in police custody and a person of interest in the murders of the high school girls created a sensation that contained elements of uncertainty, as well as a questioning of the competency of the Tallahassee Police and the District Attorney. The local newspapers carried headlines such as: "On Again, Off Again— Who Do You Trust?" and "Back to Square One." The question was being raised as to whether the local citizenry and their daughters should feel safe again. Some were suggesting that it was time for the FBI to be engaged.

Brett Gatlin had no comment when approached by reporters. Wilson Jones stated that the prosecution had additional evidence concerning Richardson that it had not been privy to before. Consistent with his promises to Brett and Roger, Jones informed them that he would continue the investigation beyond Richardson.

"Although, I'm increasingly convinced that Richardson is guilty," Jones said.

∽

Edison Peters was no longer living at the YMCA. The old single-wide trailer he was renting was situated in a trailer park on the western border of the city. All the units there were old and not in the best condition. But the rent was cheap and Edison's welfare check only provided so much that'd cover the man's rent, food, and alcohol needs.

It had been a while since Edison was near Fulbright High and he was getting antsy again. He'd stayed away ever since he got pulled in by the cops because of that Landry girl. Hah, just thinking of her boosted his testosterone and got his adrenaline pumping. Must be something in the water at that institution, but the girls there were particularly pretty and sexy.

It was time again for a little fishing expedition.

∽

"According to Wireless, Detective Jones is bringing Edison Peters back in for questioning," Roger said. He and Brett were seated together at a local Milton restaurant. "May be nothing more than making sure that he and his Department can't be accused by a defense attorney that they were only focused on Richardson."

"Maybe so," Gatlin said, "but this is something that I believe we can use to our advantage."

∽

Roger Clark was at Fulbright High going through things in the workers' locker room when Toby Parmenter showed up.

"Hey, what're you doing here? Can I help you?" Toby said.

Roger whirled about, flashed his PI credentials, and introduced himself. He was chewing gum with his mouth open, taking on the persona of a quirky guy who was careless with what he said to others.

"I'm Investigator Roger Clark working under the authority of Detective Wilson Jones, Tallahassee PD. And who might you be?"

"Uh... My name is Toby Parmenter. I work here at the school. Are... uh... are you supposed to be in here?"

Roger continued to chew his gum loudly, snapping, popping it with his mouth open. He

laughed, clapped his hands together, then signaled a thumbs-up.

"Good for you, Parmenter. That's a question you should be asking as a school employee. Can't never be too careful when it comes to protecting the students here, you know?"

Roger reached into his shirt pocket and pulled out a piece of paper.

"Got me a formal permission slip from the school board chairman authorizing me to be here at Fulbright."

Parmenter glanced at the paper, then handed it back. He'd never know if it was genuine. It was not.

"Detective Jones got me doing some checking for anything that Chuck Richardson may have left behind," Roger said. "You know Chuck, eh?"

"Know him? I worked closely with Chuck. Me and him been responsible for all the light repair work and maintenance here at Fulbright."

"Ah, so you're the dude worked with Chuck? Sure enough. Got ya pegged now. Bet this has been quite a shock for you lately, huh? First, you find out a couple of young girls from this here school end up murdered, then you hear that the guy you been working with is being accused of being the killer, eh?"

"Chuck's a good guy. You know, he's got his problems, but I have a tough time believing he'd hurt anyone. He's not like that."

Roger had his back to Toby as Roger was pulling things out of a locker that had been assigned to Chuck Richardson.

"Well, interesting you'd say that Toby, 'cause that's just how Detective Jones feels, ya know? He's got me checking things out here, because he's a thorough man. But I'll tell ya something if I can be sure you ain't gonna go blabbing this to everybody. We got us another suspect that the detective is gonna be looking at real hard."

"What? Well, that's certainly a surprise," Parmenter said. "Figured they were locked in on Chuck, you know? Why'd they switch to somebody else? You know who this other person is?"

Roger turned back to face Toby Parmenter.

"Can I trust you not to go around shooting your mouth off?" Roger said.

"Of course, I wouldn't be telling nobody, especially if it interferes in getting the monkey off of Chuck's back, ya know? I realize I'm biased when it comes to Chuck, but I been working with the guy every day. Yeah, like I say, he's got his problems, ya know? He struggles with his mind and can get really confused at times. Sometimes, he seems to even forget where he is and what he's doing, but, he's a good guy."

Roger moved closer to Toby and spoke in a much quieter voice. He reached up and placed one hand on Toby's left shoulder.

"There's this guy named Edison Peters. Last, we know, Peters was living at the local YMCA. He's got an old car. Anyway, Peters was seen hanging around the high school. The day before Michelle Landry was abducted and killed, Peters... hold on a sec." Roger walked over towards a small wastepaper basket, leaned over, and spit out his gum. "You chew on that stuff long enough," Roger said, "it loses its flavor. You begin to feel like you're chewing on a piece of rubber or maybe a tire valve." Roger laughed aloud at his own remarks. "Now, let's see. Where was I? Oh, yeah. Anyways, this here Peters tries to get the Landry girl in his car. The police hear about this and pull him in for questioning, but the guy ends up lawyering out, which means they had to provide a lawyer for him. The police let go when the guy come up with a solid alibi. Now, it seems as if the man's alibi ain't holdin' up."

Roger shrugged and lifted both hands palms up.

"Don't ask me what happened there. These detectives tend to be closed-mouthed, you know? You work with them, but they only tell you the bare minimum you need to know to do your job. Anyways, this Detective Jones says Peters may be the guy. They're bringing him back in to be interrogated now."

"Guess I'm surprised," Toby said. "Like I said, seemed to me they had a lock on Chuck."

"Yeah, well, for now, that's the way they want it to look while they come up with some more on this Peters dude. You see... "

Roger paused and looked around the room as if he needed to be sure no one else was around. "I probably shouldn't be telling you this, but you are Chuck Richardson's friend.

Anyways, once you throw Walton and Foxx into the mix, well everything changes."

"Huh? What do ya mean by that?" Toby said.

"Not sure if you remember, but another former high school student, Miriam Walton, and Lennie Foxx, her boyfriend, both up and disappeared some months back. People figured they'd run off together. Word is the police found bodies they believe could be Foxx and Walton. That's being checked out at the lab even as we speak 'cause them bodies was real decomposed, if you know what I mean."

Roger reached into his pocket for some more gum. He offered a piece to Toby, who declined the offer.

"Anyways, Miriam and Lennie, well, they both disappeared before Chuck ever come ta town, you see? In fact, let's just say that Chuck was in a place where he was not free to leave, if you get my drift. The cops recently found some proof that Edison Peters was in the area during that time. Means ol' Chuck ain't had nothin' to do with Walton and Foxx. And, if the police are right that Miriam and Lennie, Kelly Ann Lauren, and Michelle Landry were all killed by the same person, well that rules out Richardson as the killer.

Anyways, they'll confirm all that after the lab completes its testings. Lot depends on the identity of them bodies."

Roger turned back towards the locker he'd been searching and continued to chuckle.

"I tell you, Parmenter. You can't make stuff like this up, you know? It's the kind of stuff you only see on television in those crime drama shows, if you get my drift. Hey, I wonder if men like Detective Jones ever watch those shows."

Roger's chuckle extended into a full laugh.

"Well, I'm finished here," Roger said. "Nice meeting and chatting with ya, Parmenter. Keep your fingers crossed for your buddy, Chuck. He might just get through all this after all."

CHAPTER THIRTY-SEVEN

Digging Up the Past

Edison Peters was seated in an interrogation room, along with his court-appointed attorney. They were waiting for Detective Jones to join them. The attorney, Arthur Wilcox, was not all that fond of his client, but he understood the situation only too well. When the court assigns someone to him, that person is likely to be indigent and just as negative towards the attorney.

"I need you to control yourself," Wilcox said. "I'm not any happier to be back in here than you but refusing to come in would only delay things a bit. Now that we're here, we need to find out why they want to talk with you again."

Peters had his body turned at an angle instead of facing Wilcox head-on. He didn't respond to anything that his attorney was saying. His arms were folded across his chest.

Wilson Jones stepped into the room and spoke before he even seated himself.

"Thank you for coming today, Gentlemen," Jones said.

"Don't be thanking us for nothing, Jones," Peters blurted out. "You got us here again after we already been through this crap once before. So, tell us what you want."

"Fair enough, Mister Peters. You had a solid alibi last time we spoke that has since completely fallen apart. Seems that friend of yours who swore you and he were together out-of-town during both of the murders says he lied. He claims that he informed you that he was going to report this to the police. Says if that means he's in trouble with the law, he'll accept that."

Arthur Wilcox did a double-take at the news, revealing to Jones that he had no idea about any of this. He glared at Peters.

"Yeah, he told me," Peters said. "And I told him to go right ahead. He's nothing but a lying snake. He's just trying to get me back for a personal dispute we got between us. Says I owe him money that I don't. You ain't gonna be able... "

Jones put his hand up with his palm facing Peters.

"Chill," Jones said. "There's more that we need to discuss. You failed to tell us last time we talked that you'd been here in Tallahassee prior to the time that we spoke with you. You remember a guy named Lennie Foxx?"

Edison didn't even wait for direction from his attorney as to whether he should answer.

"Ain't never heard of him," Edison said. "Don't know nobody by that name."

"That's funny," Jones said, "because apparently Lennie Foxx knew you. He kept a ledger of his sales. Seems you purchased some weed from the guy on at least two occasions."

Wilcox's face was flushed. He turned towards Edison and spoke directly to him.

"I want you to stop answering questions and speaking without checking with me. Damnit, you're digging holes for yourself," Wilcox said.

Wilson Jones directed his attention to Arthur Wilcox. If it were not for the fact that Jones was in an adversarial position to this attorney and his client, he could almost feel sorry for the lawyer. Jones was convinced that if Wilcox had any choice in the matter, he would never choose to represent Peters.

"That may be the least of your client's worries," Jones said. "We've identified him as a person of interest in the murders of Miriam Walton and Lennie Foxx."

Edison jumped up from his chair. His face was red. His hands were curled tightly into fists. Spittle sprayed from his lips as he screamed at Jones.

"What're you talking about? You must be out of your flippin' mind? I ain't never… "

"Sit down and shut up," Arthur Wilcox shouted. "Do it now or I'm out of here and you're on your own."

Edison sat down, shaking his head, and mumbling a bunch of incoherent words under his breath.

"Detective," Arthur Wilcox said, "you're telling us that a determination has been made that Walton and Foxx were murdered?"

"What if I were to tell you that we found bodies we believe could be Walton and Foxx." Jones said. "They're at the crime lab now."

"So, what makes my client so interesting to you?"

"Foxx's notations in his ledger tell us the time of his last transaction with Mister Peters. It was the last entrance on the day Lennie and Miriam disappeared. We're looking to see how close that was to the approximate times of death of these two individuals."

Jones turned to Edison Peters, pointed his finger at him, and spoke. He glared at Peters and spoke with a voice tight with emotions.

"You leave the area, Peters, I promise you, we'll hunt you down no matter where you go. I advise you to take me seriously, sir. Take me real seriously."

∽

Priced at less than twenty dollars per bottle, Evan Williams Kentucky Bourbon was not only affordable given Edison Peter's limited budget, it's bold and milky taste made it easy for Peters to drink it straight. Following his time with Detective Jones, Edison was scared. Earlier, the police bought into his alibi and he was completely off the hook when it came to the murders of Kelly Ann Lauren and Michelle Landry. Now, they were linking him to Miriam Walton and Lennie Foxx. This changed everything. They'd never found anything that associated him with the Landry girl or Kelly Ann. But, based upon what they were saying now, Lennie Foxx's ledger provided proof that they knew each other—in fact, he was Lennie's last customer before the guy disappeared.

The bourbon tasted good and it was already clouding Edison's mind, but it was unable to completely free him from the torment he was under. He had to do something. He needed to know more. But, at the moment, he was unsure what his next move should be. He considered leaving town, but the detective said they'd track him down if he did. And surely, they'd make matters worse for him. Had they really found those bodies? He needed to know whether they'd really determined that Foxx and the Walton girl were dead. He couldn't eat or sleep thinking about this and what, if anything, he should or could do.

For now, Edison continued to gulp down his whiskey.

⚮

Shadowing someone 24/7 was not only a burdensome task for the police, it was an expensive endeavor. Had Dan Bradley still been the chief detective, that ploy never would have occurred. Wilson Jones signed off on it, hoping it would bear fruit or he'd know when to end it.

It was on the third night of tracking the man that it appeared as if the plan might actually work. Paul Bauer of the Tallahassee PD was on duty that night. Roger Clark was with him. When their target left his home at around 11:00 p.m., Bauer and Clark followed him. As he drove to a remote area outside the city limits and entered a heavily wooded area, Bauer called in to the dispatcher and reported what was occurring. He and Roger waited before following the man deeper into the woods. The man carried a flashlight to light his way. Bauer and Roger did not. They relied upon the flashlight being carried by the man they were following. Though it did not light their path, it did provide a sense of direction in which the man was traveling. They watched as the man stopped moving and stood in one spot pointing his flashlight all around the ground. Bauer stood on one side of the man. Roger moved around to the other side. Then, Bauer, with his gun drawn and a flashlight in his other hand, flicked the light on.

"Police. Drop the flashlight and put your arms in the air," Bauer shouted.

It was clear that the man was initially startled. Then, he whirled threw his flashlight at Bauer, and began to run away into the dark woods. He never saw Roger who threw a right-handed punch that dropped him. Roger stood over him shining a flashlight in his eyes.

"Hey, sorry about that," Roger said. "Was I in your way?"

Paul Bauer came over. Made the man turn over face down on the ground and cuffed him.

They flipped the man back over. Paul Bauer called in to the dispatcher and gave directions to the woods. The team coming would inform him when they reached the edge of the woods. Roger would remain at their current location, Bauer would go to the edge and lead the men in. Roger would have his flashlight shining to guide them. The team would have spotlights, shovels, cameras, and all else needed to excavate and search for bodies.

As Paul Bauer moved out towards the edge of the woods, Roger shined his flashlight into the cuffed man's eyes.

"Real nice of you to lead us to the spot where you buried them, Parmenter. It would have been so much more difficult for us to discover this place ourselves," Roger said.

Paul Bauer kept Toby Parmenter cuffed and on the scene until it was verified that they had uncovered bodies. It would take some time for the lab technicians to verify that these were, indeed, the remains of Miriam Walton and Lennie Foxx, but everyone correctly assumed that was exactly who these two people were.

As Bauer prepared to take Parmenter away, he turned towards Roger.

"You played me, Clark."

"No rule saying you've got to play fair with a piece of garbage like you," Roger said. "Let me tell you another little secret. I'm rooting for the death penalty for you. Hell, if that happens, I'd even try to get tickets to the show."

CHAPTER THIRTY-EIGHT

Seeking Closure

The lab technicians did establish that the bodies discovered in a shallow grave at the spot in the woods that Toby Parmenter led Bauer and Roger to were Miriam Walton and Lennie Foxx. From that point on, things moved very rapidly. A search warrant of Parmenter's apartment led to the discovery of a small bracelet belonging to Cheryl Landry that had been reported as missing by her parents, but never publicly reported by the police. In time, Detective Wilson elicited a confession from Parmenter for the murders of Kelly Ann Lauren and Michelle Landry.

Brett and Roger were sitting in a local diner having coffee.

"I received another call from Wilson," Brett said. "It appears that Parmenter's motives were sexual in nature, but the man was unable to perform. That's why with each of the victims it appeared as if their abductor began to rape them then shifted to murder."

"Frustration that he couldn't do what he wanted, I guess," Roger said.

"Exactly. Although, he might have killed each victim anyway."

"You knew before anyone that Toby was our guy," Roger said, "but you never said what tipped you off."

"When Wilson found a watch connected to Kelly Ann Lauren in Chuck's gym bag, I was convinced that Chuck was innocent. If Chuck never put the watch in the bag, it had to be someone with access. No one, other than his sister, had better access than Toby Parmenter.

Make no mistake about it, Rog, you played a key role in solving this case with the way you set up Parmenter. It was because of you that he had to go to where he buried the bodies to see if they had actually been discovered."

"And Edison Peters?" Roger said.

Brett took another sip of coffee before speaking again.

"The ledger that Lennie Foxx kept was only recently found when the police made an arrest on one of Lennie's so-called deputies—a guy named Rocky Kerfield," Brett said. "Seems that Lennie knew he'd always be a primary target for the police, so he had Kerfield keep his ledger for him. That's when the police learned of the link between Peters and Foxx."

"Aha, so that explained how Edison Peters came back into the picture," Roger said, "even though he was not the killer."

"Right," Brett said, "but the cops had known for some time from an informant that there was a substantial amount of cash that Foxx never turned in to the West Siemens Gang. That was one reason why they bought into the possibility that Foxx and Miriam Walton had run away together. Wilson believes that Edison, as Lennie's last customer, robbed him of all his cash. He left town afterwards. When he learned that Lennie and Miriam were gone, he assumed Lennie might be looking for him."

"He knew that Lennie would be in big trouble with the West Siemens thugs," Roger said.

"You bet. And, you can see why Edison Peters was so anxious to know whether Foxx was actually dead.

But I considered that we could use Peters as a decoy to help convince Parmenter that the police were claiming that they found the bodies of Foxx and Walton. When you dropped that info on Parmenter, we had him set up. He had to check and see if the bodies had been found.

"So, Miriam Walton was the first local young woman targeted by Toby Parmenter?" Roger said.

"Right, Wilson says they're still putting pieces together, but it's likely that Parmenter abducted Miriam, Lennie came upon the scene, and Parmenter killed them both.

Parmenter and his wife and family moved to this area a little more than three years ago. The police are now checking into any unsolved homicides in areas where Toby lived prior to moving here."

Roger and Brett nodded thanks to their server who filled their coffee cups again.

"Poor Chuck," Roger said. "Toby Parmenter was his one friend and the dude was trying to frame Chuck for murders that Toby had committed. Real friends are so hard to find—kind of like discovering a hidden treasure."

Brett stared deeply into Rogers eyes.

"Something I would never have known—until now."

Brett smiled as he fist-bumped Roger. Then, both men nodded at each other and smiled.

The media was hot tracking the arrest of former Tallahassee Police Department Chief Detective Daniel Bradley. The DA charged Bradley with attempted murder and obstruction of justice. It was not yet known whether Bradley would plead out for some lesser charge or take a chance before a jury. One thing that was known was that the prospect of any political future was unquestionably over for the man and the prospect of Bradley taking residence in a federal prison was extremely high.

Martin Kenworth was charged with conspiracy to obstruct justice and was awaiting a criminal trial. Meanwhile, the Fulbright High School Board voted unanimously to fire Kenworth from his position as principal.

The police suspected that Judge Frederick Van Sloot also conspired with Bradley in obstructing justice, but, at the moment, they only had circumstantial evidence against the judge. They did turn the matter over to the state judicial disciplinary commission to explore the possibility of criminal or unethical behavior that would result in the judge being impeached and removed from the bench.

District Attorney William Farragut was not charged with violating any laws. It appeared that the man simply was more interested in boosting his own career than in identifying justice. Farragut would continue to climb political ladders with his primary goal always being his own self-interest. He already had given a few interviews on national television programs taking credit for the arrests arising out of the murders of several high school students.

"By the way, Rog, when I last spoke with Wilson, he said to tell you he still plans to take you up on a day of fishing here in our area."

"Great, I'm looking forward to that," Roger said. "I love to fish, and I'd welcome the opportunity for some time with Jones."

"Speaking of Wilson Jones, there's an important lesson for you and me in all that we just experienced. Sometimes, you run into a cop who abuses his authority or, in some instances, is downright dirty. But I don't ever want to lose sight of the fact that there are thousands of law enforcement officers across this nation who are clean, do a good job, and are an incredible benefit to the general public. And, Wilson Jones is about as good an example of that as anyone."

"Man, you'll never get a disagreement on that from me," Roger said.

In addition to the satisfaction of successfully defending another client who might easily have been railroaded into a guilty verdict, the Richardson case was well-paying. Brett had structured his office whereby he, Roger, and Betty Jo Felton each received a set salary. Money in excess of salaries and benefits was retained in a fund from which additional office expenses, improvements, bonuses, and the like would be drawn. In many respects, Brett treated Roger as a partner more than an employee, although Roger, not being an attorney, could not legally partner with him.

∽

The man left the area and his pursuit of Brett Gatlin when those who hired him called him off the job. He was told that they were postponing the job, though they did not specifically state why they were doing so. He received a lucrative payment for his efforts to date and stood to make even more money than originally agreed when he went active again.

Truth is, he couldn't care less one way or another. Killing an intended target was a job, something he did, and did extremely well, for a living. Yes, he enjoyed the work, but he had no personal interest or stake in whether someone lived or died.

In any event, he'd be ready when they put him back on the job.

≪∽≫

Tara had her first look at the white sand beaches glistening in the sunshine. As expected, she absolutely loved them. Brett took her to Navarre Beach then traveled along the seemingly otherworldly Via de Luna until they reached Pensacola Beach. They browsed through the local shops, ate at a seafood restaurant, and sat on a dock basking in the Florida sunshine.

Tara wished this day would never end. Brett was more at peace than he had been in years. They watched the sun set, then walked hand-in-hand in the sand with a full moon overhead. It was deeply romantic, personal, and thrilling. It was not something easily expressed in words—it had more to do with emotions spilling out of the heart. They stopped for a moment, stared up at the sky, listened to the pulsing ocean playing its unique symphony, and marveled at the dark waters that appeared to stretch out forever. Brett turned towards Tara and gently drew her body close to his. Their kisses were filled with love, passion, and a sense that they were, indeed, soul mates destined to be together forever.

The End

Thank you for reading this book. If you enjoyed it, would you please post a review. Your support really does make a difference. Thanks so very much.

Additional books by Vincent J. Sachar:

The Nowhere Man

Nowhere Out

Nowhere On Earth

Murders at Pearl Springs

A Life Unappreciated

In the Shadows

ID: The Man with Two Lives

Cajun Culture Shock

For the Writer in You

The Lost Boy (A Christmas Story)

The Journey Home (A Christmas Miracle)

A Twisted Road

www.ingramcontent.com/pod-product-compliance
Lightning Source LLC
Chambersburg PA
CBHW072205170626
46813CB00003B/798